PRAISE FOR KRISTINE GRAYSON

"With her series of magical romances, Kristine Grayson has carved out her own special and unique place in the romance genre."

— RT BOOK REVIEWS

"The reigning queen of paranormal romance."

— THE BEST REVIEWS

"...[Kristine Grayson] will have a long and glorious career."

— THE ROMANCE READER.COM

"Kristine Grayson gives 'happily ever after' her own unique twist!"

— KASEY MICHAELS

"Grayson's clever, humor-tinged writing is absolutely delightful."

— BOOKLIST

VISIONS OF SUGAR PLUMS

THE SANTA SERIES

KRISTINE GRAYSON

Visions of Sugar Plums

Copyright © 2019 by Kristine Kathryn Rusch

First published in 2019 by WMG Publishing

Published by WMG Publishing

Cover and layout copyright © 2019 by WMG Publishing

Cover design by Allyson Longueira/WMG Publishing

Cover art copyright © Victoriaandreas/Dreamstime

ISBN-13: 978-0-615-88567-4

ISBN-10: 0-615-88567-5

VISIONS OF SUGAR PLUMS

CHAPTER 1

*T*HE TV FRITZED. Nissa Kealoha clasped her hands behind her, trying to remain calm. She could have predicted the fritz. Greater World technology didn't work well in the North Pole. Even Greater World technology supposedly modified for North Pole needs.

She stood just inside the door of the television room at Image Headquarters, suppressing a sigh. Pipe, cigar, and cigarette smoke floated around the room like a cloud. The entire place smelled like an ashtray.

Oh, how she missed New York's nanny state. She liked to breathe. But things were different here in at the North Pole. Older, slower to change. And she had to keep reminding herself of that.

She stepped through the veil of yellow smoke into the room proper. Her eyes stung. She couldn't see an empty chair. The room was filled with all of the advanced Image Specialists, the ones who refused to leave the North Pole.

Theoretically these people knew how to manage Santa's image, when in reality, all they knew was how to massage the Great Man's ego. Not that he had much of one. Santa truly was a Jolly Old Elf, concerned with children and toys and happiness. He didn't care about his brand, unless something interfered with it.

And the Image Specialists seemed to believe that this latest crisis interfered with the brand.

"Nissa," said Oskar, the head Image Specialist. Oskar had held the position for at least seventy years, after many successful years in the field. "Come join us."

He patted the chair beside him, directly across from the fritzing television screen. He, at least, had given up smoking a decade ago. Which didn't help a lot, considering how many other Image Specialists were puffing on something. She counted five cigarettes, two cigars, and five pipes, and those were the ones she could see.

One of the younger Image Specialists, a woman whose name Nissa could never remember, messed with a DVD player. Another female Image Specialist whispered something about thumb drives and internet hookups.

Nissa knew neither thumb drives nor internet hookups would work. Discounting the smoke, which had to have a major impact on electronics, the technology faced a larger problem.

The technology was made in the Greater World. This particular version of the North Pole didn't exist in the Greater World. This North Pole was in its own magical sideways universe, one that sort of *looked* like the Greater World, but *wasn't* the Greater World.

And the real techs at the North Pole, the ones who could handle Greater World gadgets, worked in Tech Toys, a protected area that separated technology from the magical energy which filled the Pole.

Nothing protected the technology in Image Headquarters. And, to make matters worse, the conference room's natural magic was considerable: the oak table had ancient spirits in it, the glass table top was made of sand from magical beaches, and the thickly upholstered chairs were spelled for comfort. The people magic was considerable as well.

Oskar was the most powerful mage in the room. He could create an image with a thought. He'd lived in the Greater World for more than a century, and had finally come back here as a reward. Nissa didn't want a reward like that. The longer she stayed at the Pole, the antsier she got.

But she did know how Oskar had become the most powerful Image mage. He'd done it through hard work. In the 1860s, he'd been the one to convince illustrator Thomas Nast to draw Santa Claus every year, a stroke of genius superseded only by the Coca-Cola ads of the 1930s (also Oskar's idea—planted in the mind of greedy cola executives).

Nissa used to admire Oskar—okay, to be fair, she *still* admired him, but she now knew that his knowledge of the Way Things Worked In The Greater World was horribly, awfully, terribly out of date.

She didn't say that as she sat down next to him. He smiled at her absently, like an indulgent father. He was old enough to be her great-great-grandfather, although he didn't look it, with his pale blond hair and unlined face. He kept himself trim, which accented his great height, something that marked him as extremely extraordinary in a world of fat elves.

She wasn't fat either. She had to stay media-perfect—American media perfect. Ten pounds too thin (just right for the cameras), athletic and toned, expertly trimmed hair, and very white teeth, "blazingly white," one of the Image execs at the far end of the table had said one afternoon. Not that he should talk; his teeth were brown from centuries of pipe tobacco and a fondness for hot cocoa before bed every night.

Most everyone in the room was white and male, except for the two fiddling with the technology and Nissa herself. Nissa didn't look like anyone else. She had black hair (most didn't), cocoa-colored skin (most didn't), black eyes (most didn't), and a smile that her mother called pure Hawaiian (thanks to her father, may he rest in peace).

Nissa fit into New York, where no one noticed how different she was. Nissa, who had a beloved apartment on the Upper West Side in New York, New York, the city so nice they named it twice. She missed both the city and the apartment more than she wanted to admit.

"How's your mom?" Oskar asked, ever so polite.

"Better," Nissa said. Her mother had severe diabetes, a heart condition, and a reluctance to get medical treatment. Nissa wanted to take her mother to the Greater World for care, but her mother wouldn't hear of it, even though the magical doctors in the Pole had done everything they could.

As they reminded Nissa every time she visited, magic had its limits. It could extend a human life, provided the human was healthy when she got the magical life extension, but magic could not prevent death—something Nissa had learned the hard way when her father had had a massive heart attack ten years ago. He'd been dead before he hit the floor, the doctors said, and then they told her that they wouldn't revive him.

To do so here, they said, would invoke black magic—even if they used Greater World techniques. All of the magical in the various magical realms were terrified of having their magic sink into evil, but here, at the North Pole, they were downright phobic about it.

Which was why she wanted to take her mother away from here to help her get healthy. At least Greater World doctors weren't afraid that normal, life-saving techniques might make them evil. In fact, Greater World doctors believed that saving lives was not only part of their jobs, but part of the reason that they were on the side of angels.

(If only they had met some of those angels they sided with; they might reconsider.)

The television fritzed again, then popped. One of the women near the screen cursed.

"Can't you just tell me what's going on instead of trying to fix that?" Nissa asked. She didn't want to be in this room any longer than she had to.

"We wanted you to see it," Oskar said. "Weirdly, it's actually getting traction, and the Big Guy himself is concerned."

The Big Guy was Santa. But Nissa couldn't trust Oskar's statement. She didn't know if the Big Guy was concerned or not. His *handlers* might have been concerned. Usually, they didn't bother the Big Guy with anything outside of the toys, children, and humanitarian concerns of the operation. He had more than enough to do every day; he didn't need branding or image worries too.

Oskar might have been the only one truly concerned, and he might have been speaking with the royal "we." Or rather, the fantastical "we," since Santa, for all his importance, had no royal blood.

"Got it," one of the women said as an image flashed across the gigantic TV screen.

The image showed a standard talk show set. Judging from the golds and yellows, this show was American daytime, probably morning, filled with "news" and happy talk. Nissa hated happy talk, and she shouldn't. Half of what she did influenced the happy talk hosts. They were Santa's biggest media supporters in the weeks before Christmas Day.

The camera panned onto a dark-haired man wearing tweed. "…unhealthy lifestyle," he was saying. He had a rich, deep voice, an actor's voice. A singer's voice. A Voice-voice, her trainer had once called it. A gift from the gods, and magic in and of itself.

Then the image winked out. The woman in front of the television cursed and bent over the technology again.

The sound continued, even though the images did not.

"…has lots of nasty habits. The examples he sets aren't good ones. Let's not even discuss the sugar, although we should, given his girth. Let's talk about the homes where he gets a glass of eggnog alongside those cookies. Eggnog, in most places, is laced with rum. And then what does he do? He gets into his vehicle and drives to the next location. After one or two of those, he's probably tipsy. Anyone would be. But I can't imagine that he would be merely tipsy. He's spending twenty-four hours plus eating cookies and drinking rum. His capacity for alcohol…"

"*This* is what you wanted me to hear?" Nissa asked. "Some rant against Santa?"

"This is not a rant," Oskar said. "We can ignore rants. This is an amazingly well-put-together argument, perfectly pitched toward America's concern with obesity and overindulgence. The country's ripe for this kind of discussion, and we all know that where the United States goes on this holiday stuff, the world follows."

Well, that wasn't true. Large sections of the Greater World didn't celebrate Christmas at all. Large sections of the United States didn't celebrate Christmas either. Nissa's neighborhood in New York had as many Jews as Christians, and the neighborhood two blocks away was mostly Muslim. She had no idea how many people in New York City actually celebrated Christmas as a religious holiday, and how many simply ignored it, letting the seasons and the seasonal holidays wash over them like rain.

But once upon a time, Oskar had lived in a rarefied United States, one that closed its eyes to differences—or discriminated against them. Nissa wasn't sure if he left before or after 1950, but it didn't matter. He missed the Civil Rights Movement, the Women's Movement, the Gay Rights Movement, and dozens of other movements.

Plus, he still had a Eurocentric Greater Worldview, something she had tried to argue him out of, and failed.

"People have made the argument this guy's making before," Nissa said. "In 2009, *The British Medical Journal* suggested that Santa eat carrots and ride a bicycle, just so that children would understand a healthy lifestyle. I'm the one who killed that story by having everyone cover it. Every single reporter laughed at it, which was exactly what I intended."

"I know," Oskar said. "Your solution was brilliant. Which is why I'm assigning you this."

She sighed, and stifled a cough as she got a mouthful of smoke. She'd have to take a shower after she left here.

"This sounds like the same kind of thing," she said. "I'll assign it to a member of my staff when I get back."

Which she hoped would be Real Soon Now. Since everyone at the North Pole was focused on Christmas, the tension here in the holiday season was outrageous. She hated the North Pole at Christmas.

New York, on the other hand, was beautiful at this time of year.

"What this young man is arguing is not the same kind of thing," Oskar said. "This time, the argument isn't coming out of a medical journal. It's coming from Professor Ryan Palmer, a deadly combination of good looks, charm, and brilliance. He's entertaining, passionate, witty, and on a damn mission."

Oskar leaned forward and frowned at the television. The Voice-voice—Ryan Palmer, apparently—was chuckling, and saying, "...yes, I know it sounds ridiculous, but we've seen that imagery impacts belief. Smoking has gone down since cigarette advertising was banned on television in 1970, and by eliminating child-friendly icons like Joe Camel, fewer young people..."

Nissa glanced around the room to see if anyone was hearing that argument. The Image Specialists didn't even smoke less as Palmer talked about smoking declining. They just clung to their cigarettes or puffed on their pipes, as if something like a Greater World Voice-voice couldn't screw up their bad habits.

"Can't you get the picture back?" Oskar asked one of the other women.

"Trying," the woman closest to him said.

Nissa tried to focus on the task at hand, which was, she was beginning to realize, letting Oskar know that Palmer wasn't a threat. Nissa didn't want to spend the holiday season arguing with some professor, as if she were his perfect foil. She had a schedule mapped out, one that would remind everyone of Santa, and would help all the charitable organizations Claus & Company had set up to deal with the other problems that the public noticed only at Christmas—poverty, homelessness, starvation (even in big countries like the US), and childhood illnesses. She loved using her position at Claus & Company to goose holiday donations.

She didn't want to be distracted from that mission.

And if anyone would distract, it would be a voice-voice. Palmer's was perfect. That quintessential American announcer combination between kind, reassuring, and authoritative. Palmer sounded like an adult version of your very best friend.

Nissa frowned at the entire idea of it.

"This Palmer is on a mission against what exactly?" she asked. "Santa?"

"No, no," Oskar said as if that were unthinkable, and it probably was. "Professor Palmer is on an anti-obesity mission, and that's a bandwagon that everyone seems to be jumping on of late. But he has a particularly interesting way of approaching it. He says we shouldn't be tolerant of role models who overindulge."

"That's not original." Nissa had heard that argument since she left the Pole and moved to New York, almost two decades ago. "And besides, criticizing role models doesn't work. America hates judgmental types."

Oskar patted his shirt pocket. She realized he was looking for a cigarette. From across the table, someone slid him a cigarette package. With a camel on the cover.

She didn't know if someone had magicked it as a screw-you to Professor Palmer, or if no one in the room had noticed that the man had even been talking about cigarettes.

"That's the point," Oskar said as he picked up the package. "Somehow this Professor Palmer isn't coming across judgmental. He's managing to come across like a reasonable guy with the solution."

She had no idea how that argument, even made with a voice-voice, could be anything but judgmental. "His solution is to make Santa skinny?"

"No," Oskar said. "The solution is to change Santa's habits. Palmer's arguing that Santa's behavior is very last century, and we need a new Santa for the modern age."

She looked at Oskar in surprise. He was staring at the blank television, turning the cigarette pack over and over in his hands.

"Do you think he's correct?" she asked.

Oskar shrugged. She couldn't tell if he was being noncommittal or if he did not want to agree with Palmer in front of the Image Specialists.

Still, she wasn't going to let Oskar off the hook.

"You were the one who made Santa's image public," she said. "It's not even really an 'image.' It's who he is. We can't change who he is from the outside."

That had been part of Oskar's genius. He had convinced the mortals in the Greater World that they had created Santa in their own image. In reality, their images just reflected the S-Elf who occupied the position.

Santa got voted in by S-Elves, just like popes got elected in the Catholic Church—only at the North Pole, the vote came a lot less often. Santas held their position for centuries, and could sometimes decree that a beloved child or heir take their place. It all depended on the S-Elf's magical capability, purity of his elf heritage, his empathy, and his political skills.

"You're not saying we're getting a new Santa, are you?" she asked, feeling both alarmed and intrigued. She'd been hearing rumors for years now that the current Santa was getting tired and wanted to pick a successor soon. She hoped that a female S-Elf would get the position, but had been informed that such a thing would never occur in her lifetime. Every century of it.

"No, I'm not saying Santa's retiring," Oskar said as one of the women slapped the television. It vibrated on its stand. Nissa wanted to tell the woman that hitting a television to make the picture clear hadn't worked in more than fifty years, but she knew she was just wasting her breath.

"Then what are you saying?" Nissa asked.

"There are a lot of competing images out there," Oskar said. "Lots of things that demand the modern child's attention. Santa is one of the few pure things left. For about ten years, a child gets to believe that magic exists. So many then get over that, and their lives become dull and sad. But those that hang on to the spark—"

"Yes, yes, I know," she said. She wanted him to get to the point. Everyone in the North Pole had been raised on this ideology. Those children who hang on to the spark become the Greater World's optimists, the ones who believe anything is possible if they only give it a try. The others, well, life got increasingly more dreary for them as the years progressed.

She'd never seen any studies that proved or disproved this theory, but that didn't change the fact that everyone in the Pole used the theory as an argument. And honestly, she loved that theory. It was one reason she worked for Image Headquarters at Claus & Company. To use Santa's good image to promote everything she cared about.

But her desire to get to the point got misinterpreted.

"Don't dismiss that idea, missy," said Ludwig, who sat in the back. He was one of the oldest of the Old Boys, a man with a long white beard, a subservient wife, and an ego the size of the Atlantic Ocean. She had always wondered how he'd managed to keep that ego in check so he could work with Oskar.

The other Old Boys also had egos, just not as big as Ludwig's or Oskar's. They all had had illustrious careers, careers she'd studied in Image class, and then confirmed (in her own way) on her days off in New York. She'd spent a lot of time in the New York Public Library, digging through old images and archives, looking for pictures of the Old Boys.

And she'd found a few, mostly in group settings like this one, holding stogies and some kind of liquor and looking very pleased with themselves.

"I'm not dismissing the argument," she said, trying not to sound defensive, even though she *had* been trying to move Oskar forward. She wanted out of this room. "I'm just familiar with it. We all are. I understand how important child-magic-beliefs are."

She probably shouldn't snap at her so-called betters. Not if she wanted to remain employed.

And while she found a lot to dislike about life in the North Pole, working for Claus & Company was one of the best jobs in any world, Greater or otherwise. She wasn't sure what would happen to her if she got fired. She wasn't even sure if she could continue to live in New York. She might have to come back here and work the toy-manufacturing line—the physical line, not the one that used magic. Her magic wasn't strong enough to work on the magic part of toy assembly. She'd learned that early. As a young mage, she'd put in her time at the physical assembly line. Even now, the idea of putting safe, plastic baby toys in gift-wrapped boxes made her shiver.

"Well, then, missy," said Ludwig. "Shape up your attitude."

She started to take a deep breath to calm herself, then

changed her mind, and exhaled. She would make it through this meeting without coughing. She *would*.

Oskar looked at her sideways, with just a bit of sympathy. Then he patted her knee. His hand came to rest on her thigh. She wanted to tell him that such familiarity wouldn't play in the Greater World, but she knew what he'd say. This wasn't the Greater World.

He'd say this was better.

And he might be right.

She frowned at the blank television. Professor Palmer droned on. Although really, she couldn't call his side of the conversation droning. Even without the visuals, he was compelling. He had to have some magic. Or supreme amounts of charisma. It wasn't just the argument alone that made him impossible to ignore.

"I'm still not clear on any of this," she said. "What does this Palmer want, exactly?"

"He wants Santa to be a force for good," Oskar said.

Well, *that* was offensive. "Santa *is* a force for good," she said.

If she didn't believe that, she wouldn't be working for Claus & Company. She wouldn't have given up her life for it.

"We know that," Oskar said, "but Professor Palmer's tarnishing the brand. We can't allow that. We must control the image ourselves."

She looked at Oskar's sincere, unlined face, and resisted the urge to remove his hand from her thigh. She didn't want to offend him, although really, Palmer and the job he represented was annoying her.

"Can't we just let this blow over?" she asked Oskar.

"Some things blow over, some things don't," Oskar said.

She'd heard that before as well. It was Marketing 101. The next thing he'd say would be that if they didn't get ahead of this train, then it would pass them by, and she would say that if they got in front of a train, it could run them over, and then they'd all argue about the use of metaphor and whether or not it was accurate, and then they'd return to the topic, and the decision would end up being the same.

When Oskar had an idea this strong, no one crossed him.

But she had to try. "I'm afraid if we give this professor credence, then the story will become bigger."

"...not even sure kids can relate to Santa anymore," Palmer was saying. "One hundred years ago, a fat, sated man was the epitome of wealth. Now we know that such a man is a heart attack waiting to happen. We associate his level of obesity with a lack of care instead of too much care..."

She closed her eyes. Okay. *That* was a good argument. Santa the Slovenly was not going to play in Peoria.

Oskar's hand slid a little too close to her inner thigh. He leaned over and blew cigarette breath on her. "*Now* do you understand?"

"Yeah," she said, opening her eyes. The television image had returned, and it now showed rows and rows of clapping people, all looking pleased. "Unfortunately, I do."

CHAPTER 2

*R*YAN PALMER SPIT the last of the mouthwash into the highball glass and replaced the plastic lid. Then he opened the little cupboard on the limo's side door and placed the entire mess in the dirty-dish box. That he knew where this model of limo stashed its dirty dishes pointed to the fact that he had spent too much of the last few weeks doing press interviews on someone else's dime, and not enough time actually living his life.

And now he was in New York. He'd recognize the city just from its sound. Honking horns, construction noise, the rush of traffic—all audible through the limo's soundproof windows. He loved the city. He'd gone to school here. At any other point, he would look out the window, compare the city now to the days when he had lived here, but not even that interested him. Right now, all he wanted to do was get to his hotel and take a very long nap.

Which wouldn't happen for at least three hours, maybe more.

The limo had pulled up in the elite section of the underground parking at one of the most famous network buildings in America. They even had had three television shows named after this place's *address*. So many famous people went in and out of here that they needed several protected entrances, even though it was New York, and all the locals were supposedly blasé about the famous.

Ryan did not want to be here yet. All the way from the airport, he'd been angling to be let off at his hotel. He figured he had an hour before he had to arrive for whatever show was on his schedule next, an hour in which he could shower, put on different clothes, and maybe, just maybe, be alone for just a few minutes.

Ryan had asked the driver to take him to the hotel and the driver had politely refused. After all, Ryan hadn't hired the driver, and drivers hired by publicists knew better than to drop an unsupervised client at an unplanned location. That was how drivers got fired and unsupervised clients made it into the tabloids.

Although Ryan didn't think he was famous enough to be tabloid fodder. *Yet,* his publicist would say. Or rather, the publicist hired by the university would say. That publicist came highly recommended, from the university's usual PR firm. The firm's usual university publicists handled the athletic department—the young kids who had no idea how to play Famous Star Quarterback or Nearly Superstar Basketball Player, not to mention the coaches and assistants who generally put a foot in something (and not always their mouths).

No, that firm wasn't used to a mild-mannered scientist who specialized in public health. In fact, upon meeting him, the publicist had told him that everything about his resume screamed *Stay Away From the Media!* Her name was Wendy ("Think magic!" she said when she introduced herself. "You know, like Peter Pan."), and she was younger than half his students, although infinitely more focused.

If it hadn't been for the YouTube video one of his graduate

assistants had talked him into making, Ryan wouldn't be "on the cutting edge of celebrity," as Wendy said, speaking learnedly about something that everyone else was taking just a tad too seriously.

Ryan could not believe the fuss. Santa Claus did not exist, except in the imaginations of small children. Santa Claus in the 21st century was a media creation that the people once known as the Wizards of Madison Avenue had created to sell cola, for heaven's sake.

Back in the days when cola had cocaine in it.

The limo driver opened the door, startling Ryan. "We're here, Doctor Palmer."

Ryan hated being called "doctor," too. He had a medical degree, but he chose not to use it. He never really trusted himself with diagnosis, and he had discovered that he hated surgery. He preferred "Professor," but no one in this weird media realm he found himself in wanted to use that.

Actually, he suspected Wendy told them not to. She thought "doctor" was a lot more impressive and added to his credibility.

Think Doctor Phil, she said.

Indeed, Ryan had replied, who was thinking of Dr. Phil, a man with a Ph.D., but no medical license. Ryan hadn't said anything disparaging, but only because he had learned that arguing with Wendy was like arguing with his C students about homework—there really was no point.

"I'm told they got clothes for you upstairs. Someone will meet you at the door and get you to makeup," the driver said.

Oh, goodie, Ryan thought, but didn't add. Because really, who said "goodie," any more anyway, at least as a full-fledged adult.

"Thank you," he said, and reached for his wallet. He was going to tip this driver, no matter what anyone said. This guy had at least been friendly.

"No, no," the driver said, waving his meaty hands. "I get well paid by your company. I'm not allowed to do the tip thing."

He didn't even sound regretful, unlike the driver in LA who had complained about that regulation for half the drive through the virtual city that was LAX. There, Ryan had been happy to raise the privacy screen.

He got out of the limo into a semi-decorated parking garage filled with murals of famous faces. That still didn't get rid of the stench of exhaust and spilled beer, but it did let him know he was in a better class of parking structure.

As if that mattered.

He got onto the elevator and closed his eyes as the door eased shut. Just a moment of alone-time, but that moment might mean everything. When this little whirlwind was over, he was going to get off the media merry-go-round; he didn't care how many books it sold or how famous he got. He didn't want to be Dr. Palmer, talking about children's health on national television and listening to fat people complain that their holiday recipes were a once-per-year indulgence and a family tradition.

A slender arm with red nails and pricy bangles caught the door just before it closed. He felt a second of irritation before the door slid back to reveal the woman of his dreams.

This woman was tall and slender, with wedge-cut black hair and almond-shaped black eyes that snapped with intelligence. Her mouth was thin and a shade of red that matched those nails. But the rest of her makeup was subtle: pre-television makeup, the kind that kept the beautiful beautiful before they became HD-ready.

She wore a form-fitting black dress that suggested but didn't quite execute an art deco design. The dress's geometric patterns actually accented the wedges in the woman's hair. She clutched a white wool coat to her chest, as if she were hot (and she *was* hot, just not that kind of hot), even though it had to be below freezing in the elevator itself. She wore strappy, high-heel shoes that made her as tall as he was, and some kind of silvery legging that suggested both nylons and leg warmers.

He had noticed all of that as she made her way across the elevator's tiny space. He was staring, and that was probably wrong. Besides, identifying her as the woman of his dreams just proved that he was exhausted. He didn't have dreams about women—except those dreams that he assumed every man had (and enjoyed) in those long days between relationships.

She nodded at him, and then did the urban-elevator gaze. It focused on the changing numbers, as the elevator climbed its way up. He was heading to the third floor. He figured a woman clutching a large tote bag, a heavy wool coat, and the latest, coolest tablet would be going up higher in this seventy-story building, maybe to one of the business floors.

Her hair moved ever so slightly revealing a small ear. It looked vaguely pointed, which, for some geeky reason, made her even more attractive to him.

He sighed, and that made her glance directly at him. He gave her a nervous smile—he was always nervous around beautiful women—and then he focused on the elevator's crawling numbers just like she did.

Finally, after what felt like two hundred years, a *ping* announced their arrival on the third floor. He shifted as the door opened, then watched in surprise as she stepped out first. He had almost impolitely shoved his way past her, assuming she was getting out on a different floor, and he was glad he hadn't. For some reason, he didn't want to seem rude in the eyes of a woman he had never really met and would probably never see again.

Wendy, darling Wendy, Wendy darling, (he sighed a second time) was waiting for him outside the elevator, her own tablet clutched against her massive (and expensively artificial) chest. She resembled a cartoon drawing of a beautiful woman next to the woman who had just gotten off the elevator. Wendy was taller and thinner, but her red hair had an orange tint that looked dyed, despite the efforts of the high-end salon that catered to her every whim.

Wendy was frowning at him and he wondered just how rumpled he looked.

"Who was that?" she asked, glancing at the back of the beautiful woman who was now walking down the hall.

"How should I know?" he answered. That beautiful woman could have been the biggest superstar in the world, and he wouldn't have had the slightest idea who she was. He followed media *trends*, but not industry gossip. He never knew who the latest, hottest star was. He'd learned, following trends as they applied to public health, that what was hot now would be forgotten a few weeks from now.

Except for the mega-trends, the mega-creations like—um—Santa Claus.

"She looks familiar," Wendy said, but not in a positive I-just-saw-someone-famous way, but in a this-could-be-a-disaster way.

Ryan shrugged. He didn't want to think about the beautiful woman any more. Which wasn't exactly true. He did want to think about her. When he conjured up ideas of female beauty. Alone. Not before yet another dumb interview.

"Is there a green room?" he asked, changing the subject.

"You're not going to the green room," Wendy said. "You need a shower, a change of clothes, and makeup. You have shadows under your eyes that children could sleep in."

Wendy, darling Wendy, Wendy darling. She was the one who had set up the brutal press schedule in the first place. Didn't she realize that real humans needed to sleep and eat and maybe sit by themselves at least once every day?

Oh, wait. He had already had that discussion with her, and she had said, *You can handle this for six weeks.* They had known each other maybe an hour at that point, and he had never figured out what made her so certain he could cope with a killer schedule.

Even now, four weeks in, she wouldn't listen when he mentioned sleeping and eating and alone time. She seemed to believe he should get up from the six hours of sleep the brutal schedule allowed him, and look camera-ready.

He wasn't camera-ready on eight-plus hours of sleep, let alone when he was jet-lagged, woozy with exhaustion, and *hungry*. That slice of pizza he'd managed to snag on the way through the airport had held him for exactly 90 minutes.

He said, "Is there food—?"

"There's always food in the green room," she snapped. "Make sure none of it sticks in your teeth."

The green room was one shower, some stupid dress clothes, and a half hour in the makeup chair away from him. His stomach was already rumbling.

If he had known the price of media fame was exhaustion, boredom, and repeating the same argument in front of a new group of (unbelievably dumb) talking heads, he wouldn't have signed on in the first place.

And, to be fair to himself, he'd tried not to sign on. The president of the university had convinced him to do this. *We're in a tough time,* the president had said. *We can't continue raising tuition. We need alumni donations now more than ever, and alumni tend to donate when someone from their alma mater becomes famous for the right things, especially things we can exploit academically. So help us out, Ry, okay?*

That "Ry" had almost made Ryan say no. No one called him "Ry." He sounded like bread. But he had agreed, because he did care about the university. And he had thought getting his message out would help kids and families.

He hadn't expected everything to focus on the three pages

in his book where he had used Santa Claus as an example of harmful media hype that needed updating for the modern era.

"Doctor Palmer?" Wendy said in that tone that he was sure she would use on a poor, defenseless husband someday. "Shall we?"

Ryan sighed a third time. *Once more into the breach,* he thought, because he knew saying it out loud would be worthless. Wendy would ask him what it meant, and then he'd have to explain *Henry the Fifth.* Hell, he might have to explain Shakespeare.

Wendy was a high-end representative of the media/publicity/punditry class. She was smarter than most, which wasn't saying much.

He'd been on a few shows where he felt like he'd have to explain who Santa Claus was.

He hoped the upcoming appearance wasn't one of those.

CHAPTER 3

*T*HE MAN IN the elevator had been unbelievably gorgeous. Magically gorgeous. So gorgeous, in fact, that Nissa worried he was a celebrity whom she didn't recognize. She'd met a lot of celebrities who could make themselves look relatively normal with the right choice of clothes, stubble, and a two-day lack of sleep. She used the word relatively, because it was always hard to hide the great facial architecture that a camera loved, blue eyes that suggested a thousand perfect summer days, and lips so kissable that it was hard for a woman—any woman—to resist.

Get a grip, she told herself as she headed down the hall to check in with the producers of the show she privately called *Made-up Controversies Are Us*. She'd been on the show dozens of times, usually in the holiday season. But she'd become a regular at other times of year, talking about retail sales and unemployment rates—only because she was pretty and articulate and had a tangential connection to those things.

If the producers truly knew who she was, she'd be on the show all the time, while they tried to get the Big Guy as the Big Get. But she used her time to plug Claus & Company, and then to remind people to donate to whatever cause was at the top of the company list that week.

Besides, she liked being the go-to girl when the producers needed something. That meant she could trade favor for favor, and get on the show when she really needed to.

She really needed to this time. She needed to deal with that Palmer idiot before he got any more airtime. She had promised the producers excellent television, so she needed to be focusing on her arguments.

Not on that incredibly handsome man in the elevator.

That was the weird thing: She saw incredibly handsome men all the time. She worked in PR, for heaven's sake, and she was on television daily during the holiday season. When she came to this place, the home of two networks (one a spin-off) spread out over a dozen floors, she saw Everyone Who Was Anyone. The big names were either doing talk shows or long-running variety shows, always here to promote their latest TV series/album/film.

She had shared a table with George Clooney in the commissary and not lost her head over his gorgeousness. (Honestly, in real life, he was a bit too thin—just like most actors. Not because they hated food, but because of that camera-ready thing.)

She had corralled one of Brad Pitt's 800 children, who, Pitt assured her when she brought the kid into the green room, was usually better behaved. She went out onto the loading dock one afternoon and stumbled on Ewan McGregor, smoking. She had been a bit stunned at just how short he was.

The thing about actors, producers, writers, *celebrities*, was that they were real people and yeah, they might be good on TV or gorgeously airbrushed in the pages of *Vanity Fair*, but they had a human side just like everyone else. They wore too much cologne or ate with their mouths open or fell asleep and snored in the makeup chair.

Even though she'd met almost all of *People Magazine's* Sexiest Man Alive honorees (if you wanted to call them that), none of them had hijacked her brain (and other parts) quite like Elevator Guy.

She probably should call him something else in her head. Or at least, try to forget him. Because she hadn't even heard him speak. She hadn't quite brought herself to say hello.

If, by chance, he was some celebrity she didn't recognize, then she would seem like Creepy Stalker Fan Girl, and that would make her horribly unprofessional. Right now, on this stupid mission from the North Pole, she *felt* unprofessional, so she didn't need to do anything to reinforce that sense of herself.

She waved at the receptionist when she reached the part of the floor dedicated to the show. "Can I go in?" Nissa asked, and then proceeded to walk to the back without waiting for an answer. The mark of a permanent guest; no one stopped her when she walked past reception.

Behind the public areas, the halls were narrow, painted a dirty eggshell, and blocked by boxes and other things some intern needed to take care of three weeks ago. She let herself into a relatively large (by New York standards) office overlooking the plaza and its fountain. Tourists milled, hoping they could see celebrities or get into free show tapings, while New Yorkers picked their way past with expressions of great annoyance. She could empathize.

The city always got crowded during the holiday season—particularly in this part, near the skating rink and the big Christmas tree and Radio City Music Hall, all those things Flyover Country had heard about since the Christmas movies of the 1940s.

Caryn Longworth, the executive producer, sat behind her desk. She had a horsey, not-camera-ready face filled with intelligence so overpowering that one look in her eyes was terrifying. According to staff gossip, Caryn was related to at least two former US Presidents, several senators, and one famous hostess from the days when women didn't serve in Congress. Caryn had the familial political brains, a rabid enthusiasm for government gossip, and a fine-tuned sense of news-as-entertainment.

Nissa loved her. They often went out for coffee together to discuss the day's TV highlights. They weren't quite best friends —neither of them felt like they were in the position to have best friends—but they would have been if they'd had different jobs.

"Please tell me this idiot professor has canceled," Nissa said to Caryn.

"Oh, Nissie hasn't done her homework," Caryn said with a twinkle that rivaled the Big Guy's. "Our professor is not an idiot by a long stretch."

"I've done enough homework to know that," Nissa said, although she hadn't been able to download any of the shows he'd appeared on. She hadn't had enough time.

"But apparently you haven't seen enough to realize that you better bring your A game," Caryn said seriously.

Nissa felt a half second of panic. Caryn had never said that to her. Caryn, in fact, said that Nissa's B game was better than everyone else's A game.

Caryn was, in some ways, her biggest fan.

"He's here then," Nissa said, pretending to misunderstand her friend.

"Oh, he's here, along with his brilliance, his beauty, and his stellar Q rating."

"What?" Nissa asked. "He has a Q Score?"

The Q Score was a metric that TV people in particular used to keep track of someone's appeal to a particular audience. Personalities with high Q Scores got more invitations to appear on television than people with no Q Scores.

Santa had a Q Score as a brand and a cartoon figure, but not as a personality. Nissa had a Q Score as a personality and it was pretty good for someone with no actual video venue of her own.

"Our professor does have a Q Score," Caryn said. "He had one *before* he ever went on TV."

"How is that possible?" Nissa asked.

"One of the most popular YouTube videos of all time," Caryn said. "You really haven't done your homework on this one."

Nissa felt her cheeks heat. "I just got assigned this yesterday," she said. "And then I was away from any internet connection. I thought he was just some anti-Santa guy."

"That's what makes him great," Caryn said. "He sounds so *pro*-Santa while being against everything that Santa does. He sounds like Dr. Oz or somebody, totally concerned with your health while basically saying you're stupid just for breathing."

"Great," Nissa said under her breath. "Too bad Santa can't rebut him."

Santa would destroy him. Charm, charisma, the ability to make someone believe that even the silliest things were possible—that was the true magic of an S-Elf. If only Nissa could get Santa here for one media appearance.

Although, she knew, that would be completely impossible.

"Yes, it is too bad that Santa can't rebut him," Caryn said. "But you'd need Edmund Gwenn for that, wouldn't you? And he's been dead since what? The 1950s?"

Nissa frowned at her, thinking for a moment before understanding the reference. Edmund Gwenn had played Kris Kringle in the original movie version of *Miracle on 34th Street*. There was quite a back story to the performance. The entire movie existed because of Oskar. Oskar put a bug in the ear of somebody at Twentieth Century Fox to do a movie about the possibility of Santa being real. The movie was having difficulties until, in a very Ghost of Christmas Present maneuver, Oskar took Gwenn to the North Pole to meet the real Santa, all the while letting Gwenn think he dreamed the whole thing.

Santa nearly blew it all by showing up at the Oscars while on vacation. When Gwenn won for his performance, Santa had shaken his hand on the way up to the stage. *Now I know there is a Santa Claus!* Gwenn exclaimed when he won, and everyone thought he meant that he was referring to the award, when actually, he was referring to the Jolly Old Elf who had just shaken his hand.

"Nissa?" Caryn asked.

"Sorry," Nissa said. "Wool-gathering."

"Well, you shouldn't," Caryn said. "You should use that fancy tablet of yours to watch what you're up against. This guy is disarming, and he's funny, and one of the sexiest guests we've had."

"It's not hard to get that appellation on this show," Nissa said, referring to the fact that most guests on *Made-up Controversies Are Us* were on the political side and therefore were not incredibly attractive by TV standards.

"Still," Caryn said. "You've got less than an hour to prepare."

"You just want good TV," Nissa said.

"Damn straight," Caryn said, "and I'm afraid this guy's going to eat you for lunch."

CHAPTER 4

*R*YAN HAD A system for getting through makeup.
He slept. Or pretended to. That way, he wouldn't think about eyeliner, foundation, lip gloss, and someone else clipping the stray hairs that had sprouted on his ears and nose since puberty. It was embarrassing and, he believed, just a bit below his dignity. Early on in this publicity ordeal, he developed the opinion that the reason TV people were so vapid was because they had inhaled makeup fumes each moment of every day.

Then he realized that he was being unfair to all the behind-the-scenes folks who were generally nice and usually as smart as his B students. It was the talking heads that annoyed him.

He got the secondary makeup room treatment, or maybe it was the tertiary makeup room treatment. He wasn't quite up on the levels of makeup rooms. He only knew that the Talent—the regular on-air folk—usually got made-up elsewhere, and The Big Names often had a makeup room all to themselves as well.

In the past four weeks, he'd shared makeup moments with aspiring models, people who'd just been kicked off their reality

TV shows, up-and-coming politicians, and other professors who seemed to make a living expounding on one thing or another.

He'd asked one professor from Fordham how he handled the interview thing, and the prof had smiled at him. *If I didn't live near the city*, the prof said, *I'd never do this. But it impresses the students.*

He didn't say it sold more books. He did say it lead to more appearances, like never-ending circles of hell, although the hell part was just Ryan's personal opinion.

And Ryan didn't need to impress more students. His best friend Jim, a constitutional law professor, said Ryan was already the campus's Indiana Jones. Ryan had objected to that: he didn't go to faraway places to steal antiquities, and he didn't look like a young Harrison Ford.

Then, a week or so after the comparison, a female student had shown up in his class with *I love you, Professor Palmer* written in florid red ink on her considerable cleavage, and he had realized that Jim was right.

Things would only get worse now.

Even though Ryan was terribly exhausted, he couldn't really sleep while someone brushed some kind of powder on his face to keep down the shine. It was all he could do to prevent himself from sneezing.

"Stop moving your eyes, Dr. Palmer," the makeup artist said. So she knew he was awake. "I'm done with them, but your beautiful lashes are getting in my way."

His girl-lashes, or so his brother used to call them. Ryan opened his eyes and saw himself in the mirror, wrapped in a protective green garment that reminded him of a hospital gown, his face half-made-up like a badly designed manufacturer's dummy.

Movement behind him caught his eye. Who should show

up, but Gorgeous Elevator Woman. She looked even better in this light.

"Nissa!" the makeup artist said. "Don't tell me you're on today?"

"For my sins," Gorgeous Elevator Woman said. She had a throaty alto voice with a touch of an accent. Scandinavian? German? He couldn't quite tell.

"Someone trying to ban Christmas?" the hairstylist in the corner asked.

"Something like that," Gorgeous Elevator Woman said as she grabbed one of the green garments. She was clearly comfortable here. Ryan wasn't. And he suspected he was the Christmas-banner that she was referring to.

Ryan sank deep in his chair. He didn't want to see her at all. Beautiful, sure of herself, and another talking head. He thought he had seen intelligence in those eyes. He had been convinced of it. He wondered what her game was.

She couldn't be a regular or she wouldn't be in this makeup room. He wanted to close his eyes again and pretend he was asleep, but the makeup artist decided at that moment to put mascara on his lashes. He hated that. His lashes were long enough, thank you very much. His *sister* envied his lashes. No one needed to accent them.

His cheeks warmed as Gorgeous Elevator Woman sat in the chair next to him. It turned slightly away from him, so he couldn't quite see her face.

"Too hot, Doctor Palmer?" the makeup artist asked. "Because if you're going to be this red under the lights, I need to tone down your makeup."

She needed to tone down his hormones. Just being this close to Gorgeous Elevator Woman was revving him up.

"I'm—okay—um—you know," he said, sounding as inarticulate as he felt. As if the day could get any worse. That's what he needed. He needed to make a fool of himself on national television.

"I'm going to reapply your base," the makeup artist said. "We'll tone you down just a bit. We want you to look pretty for the viewers."

Pretty. With his long girl-lashes and the craters underneath his eyes. Pretty with a hint of stubble. He felt the warmth in his cheeks turn to a full-fledge forest fire.

If he'd ever had any hope of impressing Gorgeous Elevator Woman, it was gone now. She would see him as a red-faced, tongue-tied bumbler, the way that all women had seen him since he first noticed the opposite sex in the sixth grade.

He tried not to sigh heavily. He tried to focus on something else. But all he could see in the mirror was his red face bobbing up from his green wrap, and Gorgeous Elevator Woman swiveling her chair to get a good look at him.

CHAPTER 5

*S*HE RECOGNIZED THE Voice-voice a second after the name registered: Doctor Palmer, hater of Christmas, Santa's arch enemy, at least this season, the professor with an agenda and a Q Score unrivaled in the ranks of professors since the beginning of television.

Nissa swiveled her chair to get a good look at him, and froze when she saw the handsome man she'd met on the elevator. The man who made George Clooney look like a starvation victim. The man who made Ewan McGregor seem hobbit-sized. The man who made her heart go pitter-pat for fifteen minutes after she left him behind.

Oh, dear. He had a high Q Score with her too. And Caryn was right: that meant trouble.

But Nissa had to play this like the professional she was. Her job rested on it. If she were feeling dramatic, she could say that the future of Christmas rested on it.

She extended her hand, thankful she'd at least gotten a manicure before she went to the Pole.

"Doctor Palmer, I presume?" she asked with the right bit of wry amusement.

He looked at her hand as if it were slathered with mud. Then he raised those miraculous blue eyes to hers—eyes that rivaled Paul Newman's in his heyday—and closed them so fast that he got mascara dust on his high cheekbones.

"*Professor* Palmer," he said, then shook his head a little as if he were uncomfortable with that. "*Ryan* Palmer. Um. Just Ryan, really, because I'm not much with formality."

He still hadn't taken her hand. She had never faced this situation before. Did she withdraw it? Did she wait?

"Nissa Kealoha," she said. "I'm with Claus & Company. I understand we'll be arguing opposite sides this afternoon."

"I'm not really a side-taker," he said. "I just—people are misunderstanding my book, that's all, and they focus on what they understand, which is Santa, and then they use it for their own ends."

His Voice-voice was warmer in person, and the humble-man act made him even more enticing. She tried to be clinical about this: He had charisma, which was a form of magic, and that voice was enough to make her keenly aware of parts of her body that shouldn't be speaking up right now.

She eased her hand back, as she slowly realized she didn't want to touch him. Touching him right now might make her combust.

She had never reacted to a man like this, never in all her years. She wanted to ask him what kind of magic he had, then decided against it. She'd learned in all her years in the Greater World that there were a lot of people here who had magic and didn't know it. She suspected he was one of them.

"I see," she said, keeping her tone as neutral as possible, "so you don't really believe that Santa has an unhealthy lifestyle."

He glanced at Susie, the makeup artist. She was watching him with bemusement. "Um," he said, that Voice-voice shaking. "I don't believe that Santa has a lifestyle at all. He is a fictional character."

"Not to millions of children," Nissa said as coldly as she could manage. "They see him as a friend, a father-figure, a magical hero. They really don't need to hear that he has troubles at home or he overeats or he's an alcoholic. I think we're spending too much time destroying the icons of childhood at the expense of childhood, don't you?"

Ryan Palmer blinked at her. The mascara Susie had put on him had flaked all over his face. "I—um—*that's* your argument? Don't you think our role models should be, well, *role models?*"

She frowned at him. He seemed to be as off-balance as she was. If she could keep him that way, she could destroy this threat in a single interview.

"And that's *your* argument, Professor? Really? Because it seems critical of children. Maybe you think Tony the Tiger should stop yelling or The Cat in the Hat should be a bit less disruptive. Maybe Sesame Street should stop showing beloved puppets living in garbage cans."

"Save it for the show," Susie said. "I've got a face to clean up and not enough time to do it."

She bent over Professor Palmer with determination.

"You're harder to make up than you look," she said to him.

Cedric, Nissa's makeup artist, powdered her face. "At least you know what you're doing, doll," he said to Nissa. "I love working on a beautiful woman who knows her makeup. We'll have you out of here in a jiff."

"Thanks, Ced," she said, and turned her chair away from Palmer. Handsome, distracting, and fake-humble. He was going to be a problem. Plus, he ruined her research time. She had planned to watch her tablet while she got made-up. Now she'd simply be showing this guy how unfamiliar she was with his shtick.

She'd have to wait until she got to the green room, and hope that Susie would take a lot of time with Palmer, so that he wouldn't join her until the show was about to begin.

By then, maybe she'd have better arguments than Tony the Tiger and The Cat in the Hat. Tony the Tiger, after all, was brand-specific, and the Cat in the Hat came from dimly remembered children's books. She needed something more current, something stronger.

And she wasn't quite sure how to do it.

CHAPTER 6

*G*ORGEOUS ELEVATOR WOMAN, whom he now knew as Nissa, was long gone before the makeup artist finished with Ryan. She had to redo his palette (her words) three times before she got it right. By then, he had ten minutes to put on the silk suit Wendy darling had provided for him, and skate into the green room.

His stomach was rumbling. He was so hungry he was woozy—or maybe that was just the lack of sleep.

Or the effects of the woman of his dreams.

Damn, he wished he could think of her in a different way. But Nissa had put him off balance from the start.

He arrived in the green room as the three hosts of this show started into a discussion of icons, role models, and traditions. A table near the door was laden with holiday cookies, fresh fruit, chips and dip, and little finger sandwiches. His stomach growled in appreciation—rather like Tony the Tiger—but he remembered Wendy's admonition: he didn't want any of this stuff in his teeth, not while he was facing the most beautiful woman in the world.

He hoped he made it through his fifteen-minute segment.

Then he'd be able to grab an apple, run to the limo, and hide in his hotel room.

Unless Wendy darling had other surprises for him.

Nissa the Beautiful wasn't in the green room. Or she wasn't in *this* green room. He shouldn't have been surprised. Several of the shows he'd guested on separated their guests until show time. That way the arguments were fresh.

He wished he had thought to use his phone to look up Claus & Company. He'd never heard of it before, although he felt like he should have. Something seemed a little off about it.

Or maybe he just wished it were off. Nissa had managed to unsettle him, and he didn't want to go on TV rattled.

A production assistant he'd never seen before, clutching a ubiquitous tablet and wearing a pair of wireless headphones around her neck like jewelry, leaned in the door. "Ready, Doctor Palmer?"

"As I'll ever be," he said with a guaranteed food-free smile.

He took a deep breath and followed the PA through the door. He hadn't even known that acronym a month ago, and now he understood that good PAs were his best friend. This PA led him around the two gigantic cameras into the small studio.

An audience awaited, which surprised him. He didn't think afternoon faux-news chat shows had audiences. He'd only seen audiences on afternoon shows like *Ellen*.

But he had long ago given up the fantasy of watching the shows before he guested on them. He was about to give up the fantasy of sleep. His stomach, however, hadn't given up the fantasy of food.

Then his eyes found the real fantasy.

She wore the same dress, but in this light, it moved like a decorative piece of art. It accented her breasts, minimized her hips, and made her legs look even longer. She had dumped her tablet somewhere.

She matched steps with him from the opposite side of the

studio. Plus she looked a hundred times more confident than he felt. She probably wasn't hungry or tired either. She looked like a woman ready for battle.

He felt like a man who needed his Christmas vacation to start right now.

The smattering of applause registered only because he saw the red "applause" light as he walked to the empty center chairs. He and the Beautiful Nissa would sit next to each other while they battled over imaginary holiday creatures. He didn't like that either.

Behind them, a green screen showed…green. He wondered what people in the booth would design as the backdrop, and decided he didn't want to know. The people in the production booth could make him seem brilliant or ridiculous with the words they put beneath his name on the crawl. They could do worse damage by placing images of tearful children facing Santa Claus on that green screen behind him.

The hosts, two men and two women, all stood. He recognized all of them from the nightly newscast. One was the in-house medical expert, Doctor Patsy Rayder, who (he thought) had a my-way-or-the-highway vibe. She was shorter than he expected. Next to her stood the show's host, Joseph Becker, a slick silver-haired talking head who always seemed to be gunning for the latest controversy.

They both reached out to Ryan as they guided him to the correct chair. He wasn't able to greet the other two until he sat down.

Next to Nissa.

Who smiled at him, and made him shiver with delight.

Dammit.

The other two nodded their hellos. The show's cohost, Adele Grippa, a tall artic blond with cold eyes, and the studio's media expert, Erik Naiten, both smiled as if they had caught him in a trap.

Ryan should have eaten a cookie, if only for the fifteen minutes of fortitude.

He'd already missed his introduction, not that he needed to hear it again. They would have rehashed the YouTube video, maybe shown a clip, held up his book (which was sitting innocuously on the end table beside Joseph), and talked about the "controversy" he was stirring up.

What he felt bad about was missing Nissa's introduction. He had no real idea who she was, and that always made for a bad debate.

Adele Grippa leaned forward, welcomed him to the show, and launched right in.

"Doctor Palmer, in some circles, they're calling you the man who hates Santa Claus," she said. "What do you think of that?"

And by the way, how often do you beat your wife? He hated loaded questions.

He smiled, hoping the smile wasn't as cold as he felt. He said, "I'm a professor of public health who used to be a gap-toothed little boy, giddy with delight on Christmas morning, hoping that Santa arrived. I don't hate Santa. In fact, I think Santa is an extremely important icon, or I wouldn't have used him as just one example in my book."

He should have said the book's title, *Healthful Imagery*, but he was feeling rebellious. He didn't look at Wendy in the audience, even though she was probably mouthing the title just to set him off.

Instead, his gaze caught Nissa's next to him. She raised one eyebrow, a skill he had tried and failed to learn after watching his first *Star Trek* episode.

"Important?" Nissa asked in that rich voice, with that sexy, sexy accent. "Do you always attack important people, Doctor?"

And do you try to stab your wife after beating her, Doctor? He was on the ropes before he even had a chance to open his mouth. Time to change the direction of the conversation, and no matter how much he disliked being here or how greatly he was attracted to the gorgeous woman beside him, he had a job to do.

"I wrote the book *Healthful Imagery* because of my concern about the state of public health in America," he said, foregoing any mention of Santa Claus at all and getting the title in, not for Wendy, but because he was annoyed. "Almost twenty percent of our children are obese. Not overweight. *Obese.* They have heart disease, diabetes, high blood pressure—the diseases of late adulthood—before they reach puberty. This is a public health crisis—"

"We're well aware of that, Doctor," Joseph Becker said as if Ryan had just pissed on his shoes. "We're not here to discuss that. We're here to discuss your attitude toward Santa Claus."

Ryan had stepped into an alternate universe. A news-talk program *didn't* want to talk about a real issue? They wanted to talk about a made-up icon? Really?

Nissa turned that sexy eyebrow on Becker, and her other eyebrow joined it. She seemed as startled as Ryan was.

"I love Santa Claus," Ryan said. "If you pick up my book, you'll see that statement on page 157."

He knew the page because he'd been in this circle of hell before.

"If you look at the index in the back of the book, you'll see that I devote three pages out of 387 to the imagery we use to describe one of our great childhood icons. The rest of the book is about the ways we can retrain our thinking to help our children grow up healthy—"

"Imagery has nothing to do with health," Doctor Rayder snapped. "Any good doctor knows that health is a collection of facts and figures, not fantasy. It—"

"Exactly, Doctor," Ryan said. He was not going to be the butt of this conversation. "That's why I'm concerned about the

12.5 million children who are obese in this country. Fact, figure, reality. It's important."

"Yet, you spend all your time attacking Santa Claus," Grippa said snidely.

"Actually," Nissa said, loud enough to quell the cross-talk. "I've been watching Doctor Palmer on his media tour. He doesn't attack Santa Claus. He questions Santa's habits."

The panel was stunned into silence. *He* was stunned into silence. Nissa the Beautiful had, after all, been brought in to argue with him, and instead, she was defending him.

"In other words," she said, clearly aware of the effect she had had on the panel, "he has a point."

"A *point?*" Grippa asked, her tone even colder. Five minutes ago, Ryan wouldn't have thought that possible. "Aren't you supposed to *defend* Santa Claus, Ms. Kealoha? Your company Claus & Company seems rather protective of his brand."

"We are," Nissa said with incredible cheerfulness. "And we certainly don't want Santa's brand to be associated with things that harm children."

"Are you saying that eggnog harms children?" Becker asked, sounding more befuddled than angry.

"Well," Nissa said, "*eggnog* usually has rum in it, and I for one don't believe in giving children alcohol, do you?"

Ryan had the urge to giggle. He hadn't had the urge to giggle since he was six, maybe younger. Some of that was sleep deprivation and hunger, but the rest of it was sheer surprise.

And relief.

He really hadn't expected anyone to take his side on national television, certainly not a woman who had brought up Tony the Tiger and Sesame Street as rebuttal witnesses not an hour ago.

"I didn't say I wanted to give children alcohol," Becker was saying.

Everyone was talking over him, and the panel was getting louder. The audience, barely visible under the lights, was leaning forward, and even the camera crew seemed riveted. But Ryan's gaze was on Nissa. She had a small smile on her face. She was enjoying the chaos.

Then she winked at him.

His breath caught. He hadn't expected that at all.

"There's no need to fight," Nissa said over the bickering panel. "Doctor Ryan is talking about very real problems in his book and on his videos. He's talking about public health, for gosh sake's, and while most people find that phrase rather dull, it's important as all get-out."

Gosh sakes? All get out? Who said those things? Maybe it was like an adult man almost saying *goodie* to a limo driver.

That urge to giggle returned. And he hadn't even had a drop of eggnog.

"I try to make the topic interesting," Ryan said to her as if they were alone over dinner. "And maybe I went too far with the Santa example. I—"

"You never go too far when you get the attention of the public," Nissa the Beautiful said. "I personally think it's time to re-examine some of Santa's brand. After all, he's all about helping children, and we certainly don't want to help them into a diabetic coma."

"No, we don't," Ryan said, "but we don't want to jettison Santa with the bathwater either."

He was mixing metaphors, but no one mentioned it.

"Actually, Santa can be very useful here," Nissa said. "The commercialization of Santa Claus has gotten worse in the last fifty years. When you think of the Ed Gwenn version of Kris Kringle, he wasn't too fat, he didn't overindulge, and he had a very gentle magic. I think if we return to that, children will still relate, and they won't get the wrong message about greed and overeating. That message disturbs—I mean, *would* disturb—Santa greatly. I think he would be happy to return to the 1940s version of his image."

Ryan frowned just a little. She spoke a bit too much like a true believer, as if Santa really existed. Although if Ryan worked with branding Santa day-in and day-out, the image might become reality for him as well.

"You're saying he's *right?*" Grippa asked Nissa, sounding stunned.

"Yes, I am," Nissa said calmly.

"Media images can be extremely powerful." Erik Naiten jumped in, clearly feeling like he needed his fifteen seconds of fame this afternoon.

Ryan was happy to let Naiten talk. He couldn't really focus on what the man was saying; instead, Ryan was getting lost in those dark, slightly upturned eyes beside him. Nissa lowered her lashes slightly, like a satisfied cat.

"If Santa were real," Becker said with startling belligerence, "why would he let any problems exist? Poverty, hopelessness, war? I know that kids ask year after year for solutions to those things, and Santa never gives them."

"Santa has magic." Nissa's tone was practiced, as if she had said this a lot. "He isn't a deity, and he can't change behavior. His magic is very specific and Christmas-oriented. He also can only work with children whose families want his presence. If the parents don't celebrate Christmas, then he's not going to impose it on them. Slowly, he's been trying to change the practice of gift-giving to help the impoverished—wishing trees, presents given through charitable functions—but he can't do everything."

"He's something we make up," Doctor Rayder said. Clearly, she was bitter about the pounding she had taken earlier. "Can't we change how he does business?"

"That's what we're discussing, isn't it?" Ryan asked. "Small changes in his personal habits. We can't make large changes in the image or more kids will get disappointed. We can't expect our fictional creations to save the world, no matter how much we want them to."

"Good point," Naiten said, and launched into some study of disappointments growing in the holiday season.

Nissa seemed to pay attention, but Ryan couldn't focus. At least, not on the discussion. It was different from all the others he'd had in the past few weeks, and he was grateful for that. It had kept him awake. Although, he probably would have been awake even with the same old discussion so long as Nissa was beside him.

A beautiful woman was galvanizing, even if she was out of his league. Even if she hadn't defended him—which she had.

"...thank our guests, Doctor Ryan Palmer and Nissa Kealoha," Becker was saying. "After the break, we'll be talking about the latest Congressional sex scandal with Congressman Polk of..."

The interview was over. Ryan could have dinner. Lunch. Whatever meal he had missed. The schedule Wendy had given him had nothing on tap until five A.M. tomorrow morning, when he'd be back in this building for five minutes with six department store Santas. It was billed as a light moment on the morning show.

Ryan didn't know if he could do light, but he could do five minutes. Tomorrow.

The red light on top of the cameras went off, and assistants seemed to appear from every corner. The audience murmured, as if they were afraid to talk out loud.

Ryan stood as Wendy appeared from behind one of the cameras. He recognized the determined look on her face, and cringed inwardly.

"Well, that was a *weird* segment," Grippa said as a makeup

assistant touched up her cheeks. No one answered her. Naiten had already exited stage right, and Doctor Rayder leaned in to Ryan.

"What *is* your degree in, Doctor?" she asked, expecting to hear he had only a Ph.D. like Dr. Phil.

"I have a medical degree from Columbia," he said with the same tone. "And yours, Doctor? Where did you get yours?"

She grunted and walked past him.

"My," Nissa said. "She's touchy."

"When people feel the need to compare degrees, they're usually status conscious," Ryan said, sounding like a pompous ass and immediately regretting it.

"Apparently, you won that fight," Nissa said.

"Nis," Becker said, almost shoving Ryan aside. "What was that? I thought you're Santa's biggest defender."

"Oh, I am, Joseph," she said. "That's why I'm paying attention to Doctor Palmer here. He's a smart man."

"Yeah, right," Becker said, as if Ryan weren't there at all. "It takes all kinds to make a show. Using Santa like that."

"If I'd known it would have brought me here," Ryan said, not caring anymore, "I would have used a less controversial example."

"You don't like being on TV?" Becker asked as if Ryan had some kind of disease. "Nis thrives on it, don't you, Nis?"

"Not like you do," she said.

Becker leaned in, shoving Ryan for real this time. "We'll get you a real segment next time. Maybe just the two of us—"

"Not necessary," Nissa said, dodging his hands.

"Thirty seconds," one of the PA s said.

"Ryan, let's go," Wendy said from her spot near the camera. He pretended not to hear her.

If he walked to "his" green room, he'd have to go right past her. So he pivoted and walked off-set in the opposite direction.

"You have your own personal stalker?" Nissa asked. She was walking beside him. Apparently she didn't miss anything.

"No," he said. "Wendy's running this tour, and I'm pretty sure she added something to today's schedule. I'm working off fumes, and if I don't eat something soon, I'm not sure I'll make it another hour."

"I'd suggest the restaurant on the lower level below the plaza, but it's a see-and-be-seen place. There's a nice pub about half a block away. Makes a great burger. A lot of news people used to go there, when there were actual reporters doing the news."

Ryan smiled at her. "Thank you. I'm not as familiar with the neighborhood as I used to be—"

"I'll walk you there. I could use a beer," she said.

She was going with him? Really? He blinked and almost told her it wasn't necessary, and it *wasn't*. But oh, it was desirable.

"I'll just grab my coat, if I can find it," he said.

"Let me come with you. I'll see if I can fend off your stalker." She smiled at him as they slipped out of the studio.

Behind him, someone counted down. "Three… Two…One…"

And then applause.

Ryan felt like a marionette whose strings had just been cut. He really was exhausted. He walked into this green room. The food here had been well noshed, but he managed two sugar cookies and a bottle of water.

A makeup artist waited. "Ms. Kealoha, would you like to remove your makeup?"

"I'm sure Doctor Palmer would as well," Nissa said, as she walked over.

He was munching on a cookie. "Ryan," he said. "Please. 'Doctor Palmer' sounds so pretentious."

"It's your name, isn't it?" Nissa said.

"I'm a professor," he said. "I prefer Professor Palmer, but

Wendy—that's the woman you're calling my stalker—she insists on *Doctor.*"

"Because she says it's more impressive," Nissa said, rubbing her face with some kind of cloth. "And for a TV audience, it is. I think you surprised Dr. Rayder when you had a real medical degree."

"Not as much as I surprised my father," Ryan said. The cookie tasted like a little bit of heaven. And it vanished in a nanosecond, followed by the other cookie.

He grabbed a third before the makeup artist gave him one of those magic cloths to wipe off his face. A shower would be good too.

"I appreciate the directions," Ryan said to Nissa, "but you don't have to come with me."

"Rethinking dinner?" she asked, and she sounded casual. He couldn't see her face, but something in her tone was at odds with her body language.

Dinner. So lunch was the meal he'd missed. Dinner sounded date-like. Dinner sounded important.

He wasn't up for important, not with the most beautiful woman in the world. "I just don't want you to feel obligated."

Nissa smiled as she picked up her coat, her bag, and her tablet. "I feel hungry," she said. "I always forget how much energy it takes to fend off Becker."

"You can say that again," the makeup artist said softly.

Ryan looked at her. She shrugged.

"Some people should be tied to a chair when they get their makeup put on," she said. "And I don't mean that in a *Fifty Shades of Grey* way."

She picked up the cloths. His coat rested next to them. He hadn't seen anyone bring it in.

"I'll waylay your Wendy woman," the makeup artist said. "But exit quickly, because I hear heels."

"Thank you," Ryan said. He blinked in surprise. "People are so nice here."

"Some of them," Nissa said. "Should we go?"

He nodded, then grabbed a fourth cookie. "For the road," he said, holding it up.

CHAPTER 7

*N*ISSA HAD NO idea what had gotten into her, both on air and off. She just hadn't wanted to hear that pig Becker attacking Doctor—*Professor*—Palmer. Ryan. (He said to call him Ryan.) She hadn't liked the way everyone was going after Ryan, even though she had intended to go after him just like that thirty seconds before.

And then the invitation to dinner. Not just anywhere either, but one of her favorite restaurants. An almost-secret place. Certainly not somewhere Becker knew about, or anyone else on staff, not even Caryn. Nissa often went there as a reward for dealing with Becker. She usually tried to escape before he could talk to her.

She usually succeeded.

Only this time, she had waited around for Ryan, like a fan girl at the stage door.

Her mistake.

And now she was helping him escape from his publicist, which probably wasn't a good idea. People like him were usually on such a tight schedule that they knocked over every single domino when they went rogue for as much as an hour.

As if that were her problem.

Her problem was that she found this guy incredibly appealing, and she had just *agreed* with him, when her mission was to take him down.

She swallowed hard, then turned and smiled at him. He was walking beside her, munching a cookie like it was a lifeline. Some glitter from the frosting rested on his upper lip, making him look a tiny bit human.

Did he realize how ridiculous it was for him to eat cookies after he had just traveled all over the country criticizing Santa for doing the same thing?

Probably not. He looked hungry. And more than hungry. He was still the most gorgeous man she had ever seen. With that dark hair, that voice, and those soft eyes, he couldn't get any more attractive—at least to her. The glitter didn't detract from his looks. In fact, the glitter made her want to run her hand along his mouth, removing glitter just before she kissed him.

Her cheeks warmed. She turned away, hoping he wouldn't see that, or at least, he would attribute it to the pace they were taking through the hallway. She reached the stairs and pushed the door open, hoping she didn't knock some research assistant aside á là *Broadcast News*.

Ryan gave one quick glance at the elevator banks not far away, and then followed her. "Good thinking," he said. "I'm not sure Wendy even knows stairs exist."

Nissa let out a laugh, surprising herself. "These stairs shouldn't be attempted in heels of more than one inch."

Yet, here she was, wearing her winter stilettos. They had a bit of padding on the inside, and reinforced toes that protected her feet from snow. Plus they were easy to pull off. But they were still stilettos.

Which reminded her. She stopped on the next landing, slipped off her right shoe, and dumped it in her bag, standing half barefoot on the cold concrete floor. Then she removed the other shoe, dumping it in her bag. She put on her slip-on boots, still stylish, but New-York-in-winter stylish, not North-Pole stylish (because North-Pole stylish involved real fur).

He watched her like he'd never seen anything like this before. His eyes twinkled, or maybe that was a reflection of the glitter.

Still, he didn't say anything, and she felt just a little stupid for wearing fashionable shoes in the first place.

She turned away, heading down the stairs. He clattered behind her. If people were listening—which they rarely did around here—they would hear the two of them coming.

Finally, Nissa burst through the door into the lobby, looked both ways, and didn't see the publicist. She beckoned Ryan as if they were spies sneaking into a summit.

The lobby was full, as it always was, with milling fans, locals, and people who actually belonged here, many of whom walked with their heads down so that they couldn't be recognized.

Nissa wasn't fooled; if the famous didn't want to be recognized, they would have used a less public entrance. She took out her day pass and ran it through the scanner, a rule she always hated—approval going in, and approval coming out.

She turned to make sure Ryan did the same thing. He fumbled with his pass, but he made it.

They scurried across the lobby, nearly bumping into the new host of the network's late night show as he carried a cardboard tray of specialty coffees just like an intern.

Great camouflage, that. She'd have to remember it for her own clients.

She slipped on her coat as she hurried through the main doors. The cold caressed her like an old friend. She held the door for Ryan, who was putting a coat over his silk suit. The coat was definitely down-market from the suit—at least $1000 down. She wondered if he knew. He didn't seem to.

They crossed the plaza, skirted the fountain (shut off for the winter), moved around the famous rink and its skaters, and went down a nearby alley.

"Jeez," Ryan said as they turned down another alley. "I feel like Harrison Ford in the *Fugitive*. The next thing you know, I'll be blaming everything on the one-armed man."

"You're cuter," she blurted, and then wished she hadn't.

"Than the one-armed man?" Ryan said. "I would hope so."

She meant than Ford, but she decided not to clarify. They reached the entrance to the pub—or at least, the stairs leading to the entrance. It was on the basement level of another large skyscraper, and the pub's owner paid for the outdoor entrance at his own expense.

He also kept it up—no ice on the stairs, which, considering this winter already, was pretty impressive.

She always felt like she was entering Cheers when she went in, even though she knew that fictional bar was in Boston. The angle was the same, though, and every time she entered from the deep cold to the enveloping beer-scented warmth of the wood interior, she half expected someone to shout "Norm!"

"Nice," Ryan said as they stepped inside. "This has been here a while. I wonder why I never knew about it."

"Most tourists don't," she said.

He gave her a disparaging look, and she suddenly remembered his tone with Doctor Rayder. He had gone to Columbia, which wasn't that far from here.

"And," she added, hoping to cover her mistake, "impoverished medical students probably couldn't afford this place."

"Nice try," Ryan said with a smile, "but you didn't quite pull away from the faux pas."

He looked around, while she grasped for something to say.

Then he added, "I suspect impoverished professors can't afford this place either."

"Professors who wear silk suits should be able to afford anything," she said.

He looked sheepish. "The university is fronting the publicist, and I assume they're paying for the clothes because I'm not. I was told I couldn't go into public looking like a refugee from the 1990s."

"Is that the last time you bought a suit?" Nissa asked as she grabbed two menus and led them into the dim darkness at the back. The best tables were near the gas fireplace, not because it was warm, but because it was private.

"I don't remember the last time I bought a suit," Ryan said, pulling a chair out for her as if he did that for women every day of his life. "But I do remember the last time I *wore* a suit. It was for my brother's wedding, and the damn thing was purple."

"The wedding?"

"Almost," he said. "Their colors were purple and white."

"Like TCU?" she asked.

"Like Northwestern," he said. "Where they met."

"Uck," she said. "I'd have to get married in Christmas colors."

He looked at her in surprise. "I didn't think there were schools with red and green."

"Not famous ones," she said, covering.

"Well, I'm not getting married in Columbia blue and white," he said, looking around. "Should I go up and get us something to drink?"

"Someone'll be here in a minute," she said.

"Let's hope the cookies hold out that long," he said.

Nissa grinned and slipped him a tin of bar nuts. "You know, I should have taken a picture of you eating those cookies."

He smiled. Which softened his face, and made him seem less handsome, more approachable. "I never said there was anything wrong with cookies."

"Yes, you did," she said.

"No," he said. "I think cookies, like everything else, are fine in moderation."

He slid the bar nuts back toward her.

"Not feeling moderate about bar snacks?" she asked.

"I had a friend who used to sneeze in those. Deliberately," he said.

"Oh," she said. "You've had some lovely friends."

He grinned. "I could lie and say the 'he' in question was my brother. But that's not true. Those friends were mostly *like* my brother. Or my students, if you prefer."

She heard something wistful in his voice. She was good at tones. She frowned. "Are you homesick?"

He shrugged, but his gaze no longer met hers. Then he shook his head, as if he were having a conversation with himself. "I...this sounds so stupid."

She waited. She'd learned long ago that responding to a statement like that would derail the conversation.

"I..." he sighed. "I didn't know what I signed on for."

"The travel?" she asked.

"The insanity." He looked up at her. "I know you work in this profession, and I don't mean to insult you, but everyone seems to be trying to gin up a controversy, and then when they have that controversy it rises to new levels of crazy as the time goes on. I mean, we're talking about Santa Claus as if he's real."

She stiffened in spite of herself.

"To millions of little children, he is," she said. Not to mention that he *was* real, just not quite in the way the rest of the world thought.

"I know, I know," Ryan said. "And had I known that using him as an example would turn my life upside down, I wouldn't have done it."

She leaned back just a little, feeling confused. "Don't you believe what you've been saying? Don't you believe that Santa's image is hurting children?"

His right hand clenched for just a moment, and then it relaxed, almost as if it had never happened.

"I *never* said that." His voice was calm, despite his physical reaction. "I *said* that Santa's image needs to be revised with the modern era in mind—and you defended that position not an hour ago."

Nissa felt the heat in her face increase. She hadn't blushed like this in years. If ever. He was right; she had defended that position, and it could get her into a lot of trouble.

She had had a moment of panic, thinking he didn't even believe what he had been saying, when she had put so much on the line. She had misunderstood.

A waitress hovered over them. Nissa hadn't even seen her arrive.

"I need a burger," Ryan was saying. "Charred. Grilled to death. So well done that we all know the damn thing is dead. And instead of fries, a salad, up front if you can do that."

"A burger, Mr. Health Nut?" Nissa couldn't help herself. She found his food choices amusing, especially since he was so judgmental about Santa's.

"That's Professor Health Nut to you," Ryan said, "and I indulge at times. I even stress-eat. I'm aware of it, and I'm trying to deal with it. But I give myself some treats on days like today. I bow to the public health concerns by eating the burger well cooked. No e-coli for this guy."

"Or for anyone else here," the waitress said, sounding offended. "We get hundreds on our health inspections, and before you open your tourist blowhole again, we don't pay for those rankings neither. We run a clean place."

Ryan looked startled. Nissa felt bad for him. She hadn't meant to open that door. She didn't want everyone to pile on.

He said to the waitress, "I wasn't implying that you ran a dirty restaurant. I'm just—"

"Oh, you was implying it," she said. "You was actually kinda stating it. You like this guy?"

She asked that last of Nissa, whom she obviously recognized as a regular.

"I just met him," Nissa said. "But I do—"

"And you brung him here, la-di-frickin-da. Ain't we lucky?" The waitress sighed. "He's this fussy about a burger, you gotta wonder what he's like in the sack, you know?"

Oh, Nissa did wonder. Nissa had to work to keep from looking at Ryan. She wasn't sure if this would amuse him or insult him more.

"You having your usual?" The waitress asked.

"Yes," Nissa said.

The waitress pointed the pen at Ryan. "And you. That burger'll be dead. I promise."

She stalked off. Ryan shook his head, and then put a hand over his forehead. He looked exhausted.

"I'm sorry," Nissa said. "I didn't mean to start that."

"I'm so tired that I don't know what I'm saying half the time. I'm not—fussy—usually, just—God, I've missed New York."

Nissa blinked. She hadn't expected that. "What?"

He let his hand drop. He was grinning. "People here say what they think. In the real world anyway. In the TV world, it's all about the controversy, but here, you know where you stand."

He looked at the swinging kitchen door, and his smile grew wider.

"And there's nowhere I'll ever be able to stand that will impress her. If I come here for years, she'll give me an over-cooked burger, and she'll give me crap about it."

Nissa smiled too. "Yeah, she will. Let's just hope the burger's not tough."

"In a good restaurant, well-cooked hamburger will be just

as good as undercooked. And if it's not, I'm ready to eat the bar nuts. I don't care who sneezed on them." His grin faded. "I'm sorry I sound like a pompous ass. I'm dying of hunger. Except for cookies and a slice at the airport, I've eaten nothing since LA."

"You started in LA this morning?" That was a long flight by commercial air, and if the publicist treated him the way that others got treated, he was in coach. He might have gotten cocktail peanuts or some kind of truly bad sandwich, but little else.

"Yeah, I was in LA. My day started at four A.M. One four-thirty A.M. interview, live on camera, another on tape for the eight A.M. show, and then a radio appearance on the way to LAX."

She did the math. He must have cut it close. Because to get to New York in time to be on *Made Up Controversies Are Us*, he had to be on a flight by seven A.M. at the latest.

"I slept on the plane. It didn't do a lot of good. Some kid kicked my seat for the whole five-plus hours of the flight. Or maybe it just seemed that way." He sighed. "I'm sorry. I'm not usually a complainer."

"Maybe you should be," Nissa said. "This sounds ridiculous. No wonder you're stretched to the breaking point. When are you done?"

He sighed. "What day is it?"

"December third," she said.

"Oh, crap. I have another week." He looked even more tired, if that were possible.

Poor thing. She would have revolted long before this. "Then you get to go home?"

"Then I get to go home just in time for the last week of classes, and exams. I'm sure I'll get lots of ribbing from the students, lots of debriefing from the faculty." There was that wistful note again, as if he couldn't wait. He seemed to love teaching.

She tried to find an upside for him. "At least your book hit the *Times* list."

He gave her a wry smile. "And how many people will read the entire book when they realize it's not about Santa Claus?"

Good point. She shrugged, even though she knew the answer. So did he. The book would languish on coffee tables until the next controversial book hit the airwaves.

"You'll make some money," she said. She wasn't quite sure why she was trying to make him feel better about all of this. Maybe because he looked so tired, so defeated.

"I'm not in this for the money." He grabbed the beer nuts and shifted the container from hand to hand. "I actually want to educate people. Our food is killing us. Additives and unnecessary ingredients, and corn starch, and overeating—"

"I know," she said, realizing why the publicist had focused on Santa Claus. Ryan really *was* on a mission; just not the one the Old Boys thought he was on. "I read the news."

"Which means you don't know," Ryan said. "Do you know anyone who's overweight? Got chronic health problems like diabetes? Or gout? Did you know those used to be rich people diseases? And they're infecting kids now? This is a crisis—"

"Soapbox alert," she said, holding up her hands. "I *agreed* with you, remember."

"Sorry." He let go of the beer nuts. "This is what I've been wanting to talk about, and whenever I do, everyone runs from the topic. They don't want to hear about it. I get it. I do. But I've been wanting to have a substantive discussion with *someone* for four weeks now."

"I'm your designated someone?" she asked with a smile.

"Yes," he said. "Yes, you are. Do you mind?"

She did, a little. She wasn't sure why she had asked him here, except that she had found him attractive and smart and sexy. And now he was revealing himself as a professor of public health. The kind you didn't want to go on a tear.

"Are you sure you want to have this conversation with me?" she said. "I work for a company called Claus & Company. I *like* Santa, as much as I agree with you about modernizing him."

"I don't dislike him," Ryan said, looking like a man who wanted to bang his head on the table. "I—"

"I know," she said. "I'm sorry. It's just I'm not the person you should be talking to."

Or maybe she was. Because his speech hurt a little, which was why she tuned him out. Her mother had loved her baked goods, her cookies, her candies, and just plain eating. And her mother hated exercise in all forms, not that exercise was easy at the North Pole. You had to like winter sports, from ice-skating to cross-country skiing to snowshoeing. Her mother hated all of that, and lived for her allotted month off in the Hawaiian Islands. Where the eating habits weren't a lot better than the North Pole, but at least in the Islands, her mother walked everywhere and waded into Pacific and took diving lessons back when Nissa was a girl, a long, long, long time ago.

That was where her mother had met Nissa's father. Food had been their way to relate. And they both related themselves into larger and larger sizes. Her father had died young from something preventable. No magic there, either.

Ryan was watching her. It was almost as if he could see those thoughts run across her face.

Maybe he could. She had fought her own weight for years now, probably making a different sort of bad choice, not eating enough instead of eating too much.

"I'm sorry," Ryan said. "You've been really nice to me, and I've been sticking my foot in my mouth all afternoon. Let's stop talking about me. I really do want to know about you. You're the first real person I've talked to in weeks."

She wasn't that kind of real. She wondered what he'd think if he discovered she was from the North Pole. *That* North Pole.

"Please," he was saying. "Tell me what you do for Claus & Company?"

She would love to. She would love to tell him everything, including how magic failed at the most important levels. She would tell him about the importance of happiness—how she was in the happiness business—but maybe that business needed some tweaking.

She would talk to him, professional to professional, and maybe, *maybe* woman to the man she was attracted to, and—

None of that was going to happen. She couldn't let it happen. She'd only known him a few hours.

"We manage Christmas brands," she said, telling what little part of the truth she could. "Including Santa. So I am intrigued by all of this."

His smile looked pasted on, rather like it had on the show an hour before. He knew she was skating over everything. He probably thought she didn't like him.

And she did. She really did.

"How do you get a job like that?" he asked.

She let out a small laugh. No one had asked her that before. "It's a family business. I showed an aptitude for Greater—um, for the media, and branding, and ended up in New York. I love it here."

"The company has offices outside of New York?" He frowned at her.

"You'd be surprised at how big this company is," she said.

"I'm not sure I would, given what I've been through lately," he said.

The waitress came by and dropped the salad in front of him. The lettuce bounced twice before it settled. He thanked her, but she had already left before he got the words out.

"It sounds like you need a break from all things Santa," Nissa said.

"If you're all things Santa, then no, I don't need a break," he said. "You're the nicest person I've meet in weeks."

She smiled. Maybe he wasn't attracted to her, but at least he found her likeable. That was a start, anyway.

Not that she knew what it was a start of. If anything. He was a professor, after all, and she had a weird job.

And a very weird life.

"Still," she said. "Let's talk about something else. How about them Mets?"

He laughed, just like he was supposed to, proving that he truly was a New Yorker at heart. She wished she could have a real conversation with him.

She usually didn't wish that about anyone. She liked keeping the family secrets. But not today. Today she wanted to give him just a little bit of magic, something else to believe in.

And giving away that kind of information was something she could never ever do.

CHAPTER 8

*T*HEY ACTUALLY TALKED baseball in the middle of the Christmas shopping season. They couldn't talk football because he was too addled and stressed and time-challenged to keep track of the games like he usually did (and he refrained from telling Nissa that he was concerned—as a doctor and a professor of public health—about enjoying a sport which damaged its players horribly for life).

Nissa got some kind of grilled chicken sandwich and ate it slowly. He had finished his burger so fast that he must have sent some sort of land-speed record. The burger had been delicious, even though it was charred an inch past its natural life, and he now knew why Nissa frequented this place.

He was trying hard not to be a spoilsport, trying not to be that pedantic guy you invited to your house only to realize he could talk about three things well, and on everything else he was a judgmental idiot.

The problem was that Ryan felt like a judgmental idiot whenever he was tired, and he had gone beyond tired around Thanksgiving. Which seemed like years ago. Thanksgiving had been his last day off. He had been "given" that day to spend with his family, although Wendy had called in the middle of dinner to ask if he would do a live remote from his brother's library for some newscast.

Ryan had somehow missed Wendy's call. He got the rather irate voicemail five minutes after he hit "ignore," and decided then and there that "ignore" was his very best friend.

Thinking of which, he groped for his phone. Wendy should have been trying to call him. He should have been pressing "ignore" every fifteen seconds.

"Everything all right?" Nissa asked.

"I think I left my phone at the studio," he said, and then he laughed. "No wonder Wendy can't find me. She probably put tracking software on the damn thing."

"She's dedicated to her job," Nissa said.

"I'm told she's the best," Ryan said.

"You don't believe it?" Nissa asked.

"I don't know this world, and I don't really want to."

"That was polite."

He shrugged. "I'm not cut out for this."

"Actually," Nissa said softly, "you are. You're handsome and personable and you make even the most difficult subjects understandable—"

"That part comes from being a professor," he said, feeling a bit uncomfortable at her description.

"Oh, no," she said. "I've known a lot of professors. The good ones make things clear and fascinating. The bad ones make you never want to discuss a topic again."

He chuckled, remembering an econ professor he'd had who was so stunningly bad that the dense and dry textbooks seemed twice as entertaining.

"Okay," he said. "Point taken."

"Really," she said. "You've got more charisma on camera than anyone I've seen inside the business let alone outside of it. Your voice is very persuasive. Do you have ma—?"

She stopped herself, as if she were about to say something untoward. He wondered what that would be.

"Is that why you defended me? Because I'm persuasive?" he asked, thinking maybe he would make that into a joke, but by the time he'd finished the thought he knew it wasn't.

"No," she said firmly. Then frowned. "Maybe. Actually, I think we agree on some of this, and I do want to take it to my people."

"They can change Santa's image?"

She looked at him sideways, and for the first time since the elevator, he noted her slightly pointed ears. He *was* tired. Was he thinking she was some kind of elf?

A woman who had pointed ears who worked for Santa. He knew he wasn't hallucinating her because his stomach was full and he was in a pub that he could never have found on his own. He had had no alcohol, so he wasn't wearing beer goggles.

She was real. He was tired. He imagined things when he was tired. He just had to leave it at that.

"We can try to change Santa's image," she said after a moment. "Not this Christmas, though."

"By next Christmas, I'll be yesterday's news," he said. He *hoped* he would be. Because he couldn't do this one more time. He just couldn't.

"I know. But Santa's image isn't a one-season thing." She spoke softly, as if she were talking to herself. Then her gaze met his. He felt like she had touched him. There was something alive in her gaze, something he liked, something—

Oh, jeez, he was tired.

"I would like to see you again," she said, and he couldn't tell if she was speaking as a woman or as the public relations person for Claus & Company. Not that it mattered. He didn't have time to sleep, let alone spend a day with a beautiful woman.

"I'm so booked," he said, and he hoped it didn't sound like

an excuse. He really wanted to be with her. More than he could say.

"I know you're booked," she said. "I didn't mean now."

He blinked. A date? She was asking for a date? Or was this professional? And how did he ask that without being really clueless?

"Let me contact you after this tour thing ends," she said. "Do you have a card?"

He did, now, even though he had been tempted to toss them all. Wendy had drawn them up for him when she realized he didn't have one.

What professor needs a business card? He had asked.

You, Wendy had snarled.

He fumbled for his wallet. He had a moment of panic as he worried that he'd left his wallet with his phone, but he hadn't. The wallet was with him; the phone wasn't. He smiled to himself. Yeah, that wasn't intentional. Nope, no sir, no way.

He pulled out a card and handed it to Nissa.

"I'm getting dinner too," he said.

"No," she said. "I invited you."

"And I'm not paying for anything on this trip. Let me."

"Yeah," the waitress said from behind him. "Let him."

She snatched the credit card out of his hand and vanished with it. He hadn't even seen the bill, and he wasn't sure he cared.

"Here's my card," Nissa said, and handed him something done in tasteful green and gold. He never normally would have thought green and gold tasteful, but these colors were muted and the gold seemed to sparkle all on its own.

The card just had her name, Claus & Company, a phone number, and a corporate e-mail.

He turned it over as he put it in his wallet, hoping for a private number on the back, but no such luck. No date then. Just business.

"You think I can help you with rebranding Santa?" he asked.

"I want to read your material and develop a few things," she said. "Then I need to talk with some important people. Maybe after the first...?"

If I survive to the first, he thought but didn't say. "I'd like that," he said. "I'd like that very much."

CHAPTER 9

*N*ISSA WALKED HIM back to the plaza, figuring he could find his way inside again. She thought she might take him upstairs to search for that lost phone, but that felt just a bit off.

He looked so tired. He needed sleep more than he needed—what had he called it?—a real conversation. She wished she had the kind of magic that would give him just a little energy boost. But her magic was subtler than that. It made people trust her. She could design beautiful imagery and convince people to spend money where they normally wouldn't.

In the off season, in fact, she designed brochures for some of Santa's favorite charities, as well as websites and giving campaigns. Just a touch of magic to convince someone to click the "donate five dollars" button or text the right combination of letters to the designated number. Her campaigns always brought in more money because of that hint of magic.

Not enough to convince people to spend money they wouldn't normally spend, but just enough to relax them, to make them think they were a tiny bit better off than other people. Enough to make them confident in their own ability to change someone's life for the better.

She probably could have given Ryan that kind of boost, but she hadn't thought of it until she watched him stagger inside the building. And even then, the idea felt just a little wrong. She didn't want to magick him in any way. She wanted him free of any influence, even the slightest influence.

Then she sighed, her breath frosting in the chill night air. She could hear the music from the skating rink, the laughter of lovers and tourists who were having their ideal Christmas.

She liked this guy way too much.

Now she would have to go home and tell everyone in the North Pole why she hadn't reined him in. Why she had offered to meet with him in January.

Why she *wanted* to meet with him in January.

And she couldn't even tell the truth about it, because she wasn't entirely sure of the truth. Yeah, he had good ideas. But he had even better eyes. She could lose herself in them.

Or maybe, she already had.

CHAPTER 10

*T*HE MEAL OUT had been worth the look Wendy, darling Wendy, Wendy darling had given him. Hell, the meal out had been worth the entire trip, with all of its hassles. And that was saying something.

It had even relaxed him about Wendy darling.

She had been marching around the third floor, searching for him, clutching his phone in one hand as if squeezing it would conjure him up.

Then, when Ryan appeared, she had squinted and yelled at him for leaving without her, for blowing the schedule, for being impossible to find.

Network employees watched. He had a hunch the encounter was being filmed. It might even end up on YouTube —or it would have if he had said what he was thinking.

Instead, he said meekly, *I need to eat sometime, Wendy. I just went for a meal.*

I have a meal scheduled for you after you get to your hotel, she snapped.

Good, he said. *I'll probably be hungry all over again. You know, you really need to set up these tours with human beings in mind. We need food and sleep to function at even half capacity.*

And then he had walked off, taking the elevator down to the parking garage where he had gambled that the limo was waiting for him.

He had been right. Same driver, same limo. And when Ryan asked if he could leave without Wendy, the driver smiled and said, *Why not?* as if it had been his idea.

It took less than ten minutes to get to the hotel, less than twenty to have a shower and turn down the sheets on the bed. Less than thirty to realize Ryan wasn't going to sleep no matter how tired he was.

Visions of Nissa were dancing in his head.

The woman had charmed him. He liked her more than he had liked a woman in years. Not since Claire in college. He'd lived with Claire for a few years, before they realized that they didn't belong together. Claire had been a wonderful person, and now she was one of the best pediatricians in the five boroughs, but they'd never had that spark.

Ryan got out his wallet and slipped the card from it. He was so tired that the words seemed to dance, the gold seemed to spark. He could see little flakes of magic float around his fingertips, as if the card gave off the essence of Nissa.

He smiled at it, then closed his fist around it, and leaned back.

This time, he fell asleep—and his dreams, well, his dreams were the best dreams he'd had in weeks. Maybe years. Maybe in his entire life.

They almost made the four A.M. wake-up call worthwhile, even when he realized he wouldn't have time for room service breakfast. Even when he heard that Wendy, darling Wendy, Wendy darling had squeezed in another interview right over lunch.

He wished he could see Nissa again, and he was sorry—oh so sorry—that he had to wait until January.

Because at this rate, he was beginning to wonder if January would ever come.

CHAPTER 11

*C*HRISTMAS PASSED IN a blur, just like it always did. No one at the North Pole got to celebrate in December. For a while, they tried to celebrate in January, but realized they were all too sick of the season to even pretend they wanted gifts or candy or Christmas trees. Christmas for the folks at Claus & Company took place in late May/early June, almost as incentive to get back into the festive spirit.

Usually Nissa loved those celebrations. But this year, she worried about them, since her mother was still not well.

Like everyone else at the North Pole, though, her mother had done what she could to get through Christmas. And Nissa took care of her and filled in where she was needed, which was usually Last Minute Toy Creation, something she wasn't half bad at—something to do with imagery and good feelings and all those little things her magic could manage.

She hadn't minded the whirlwind end to the season because it prevented her from thinking about anything except toys and snow and holidays. Even her mother's mood had lifted.

Nissa hadn't had much of a chance to think about Ryan, either, nor had she used any of the Pole's spying capabilities to keep track of him. That had taken a lot more restraint than she had expected; after all, she had only met him the once.

But she felt connected to him. She also felt a bit stalker-y. Before she had come home to do her stint in the toy mines, she had downloaded all of his interviews. She watched them one by one, sometimes over meals, sometimes before bed. (Too often before bed.)

If someone had asked her what she was doing, she would have said that she was doing her research for her debrief after the holidays. But no one asked. She wasn't even sure anyone noticed, although once her mother had found her, sprawled on the couch staring at her tablet, and asked, *Who is that nice-looking young man?*

Nissa wouldn't have called him *nice*-looking, which she saw as a step down from *good*-looking, nor would she have called him *young*. She would have called him *perfect*. But she didn't tell her mother that. Instead, she had said, in the most noncommittal voice she could manage, *He's a professor of public health at some university.*

Too bad, her mother had said. *I thought maybe he was someone interesting.*

Oh, how Nissa wanted to correct her mother. Oh, how she wanted to talk to her mother. But Nissa had no idea what would happen with Ryan down the road, and she didn't want to get her mother's hopes up. Her mother had wanted Nissa to get involved with someone for years now, and so far, that hadn't happened.

Not since her second year in New York. Year One had been all about dating a bunch of good-looking (*nice*-looking?) but somewhat creepy men. Year Two had been about Adam, who had been fascinating at first, mostly because he wasn't creepy, was totally brilliant, and didn't believe in any of that "fantasy crap," as he called anything to do with magic.

Ultimately, though, his dismissive attitude—which was

probably what had attracted her—repelled her. His brilliant mind remained closed to most everything he didn't understand. If he couldn't prove it, it didn't exist. And after a while, that had grown truly wearing.

Not that her mother had met him either. As far as Nissa's mother was concerned, Nissa had never had a serious relationship and really needed to lay off work for a while.

Nissa always felt like she needed to lay off work after the holidays. She felt that way now, as she approached the debrief.

Because she knew it would be ugly.

For one week after she had seen Ryan, he had continued to talk about Santa and Santa's bad habits. No one from Image Headquarters had called her, which seemed even more ominous than a what-the-hell? phone call.

By New Year's, she wondered if she would be relegated to the land of last-minute toys forever.

And now, she would find out. January 2. D-Day. The day that would live in infamy.

The day that could, she feared, change her life forever.

CHAPTER 12

*S*CHOOL DIDN'T START for one more week, but Ryan was in his office already. He had retreated here after returning from the Trip From Hell, which was the only way he referred to the book tour now.

Yes, he had made some extra money, and he had gotten in the virtual Rolodexes (if people even called it that anymore) of more than twenty major talk show producers. Some had already called him for "public health's take" on gluten-free foods or the latest flu epidemic.

He'd begged off, in one case pleading flu himself, even though he was remarkably healthy, considering what a pounding his body had taken in the height of cold-and-flu season.

At the end of the final week, Wendy'd had to leave the tour because *she* had contracted flu, and he'd actually sent her flowers, along with a large delivery of the best chicken soup in New York City. He tried not to see the delivery of the soup as a kind of middle-finger toward her; he wanted to feel compassion, but he really didn't. Wendy had made his life miserable for six weeks, and while he knew she was only doing her job, he still felt rather angry about it.

And gun-shy. He didn't want to talk to anyone. End of the semester classes, which he had been looking forward to, felt like running some kind of gauntlet, and Christmas shopping, with its tinny Muzak and cheerful salesclerks, gave him talk-show flashbacks.

At least the family Christmas dinner had been nice. Until his nephew showed a composite of all of Ryan's interviews, proving his suspicion correct. Ryan had restated his position— if, indeed, anyone could have a real position on Santa Claus— so many times that he actually had used the same phrases over and over again. It looked like one of those joke videos, and to his family it was.

To Ryan, it was just another aspect of his nightmare.

The only thing that had gotten him through the nightmare had been that lunch/dinner/meal with Nissa Kealoha. He fell asleep those last seven nights with her business card clutched in his hand. The card should have fallen apart, but whenever he looked at it—and he still looked at it daily—it seemed brand new. Sometimes he thought maybe it replenished itself in his wallet.

But he knew that wasn't possible. She had just had it made out of the sturdiest paper known to mankind. Or something. If he were a business card kinda guy, he would have asked her where she got the cards printed. But he hoped he would never need a business card again.

He was holding that card now. He was sitting at his desk, piled with paperwork that had stacked up while he was away, and he was turning a little green-and-gold business card over and over in his hand. Then he would look at the solid black phone that had been on this desk since the Reagan Administration, and he would wonder if he should pick up the receiver and dial Nissa's number.

He wanted to use the ancient landline, connected to the university's system, because—for some reason he couldn't quite name—he was embarrassed to use his own cell phone. Maybe because he knew that Nissa wanted to keep their relationship professional, and to him, the relationship wasn't professional at all.

He'd even watched their interview. His responses were cringe-worthy (although he always found his interviews cringe-worthy) but her defense of him was spirited. She had looked surprised at herself, as if he had convinced her of the importance of his argument, even though he couldn't seem to convince anyone else about it.

He set the card back in his wallet and tried to concentrate. That little blip in his life was over.

Ryan got up and walked to the mullioned window that overlooked one of the most beautiful sections of campus. Evergreen trees, ancient buildings, lots of walking paths—all covered with snow right now, since it was deepest, darkest winter in Upstate New York. But he loved it. He loved the time of year; he loved the quiet.

Or he usually did. Right now, he was restless. He hadn't been able to concentrate since he returned.

And he blamed that business card.

He wanted to call Nissa, but he wasn't exactly sure how to approach her. If he should approach her at all.

CHAPTER 13

*S*HE SHOULD HAVE brought a gas mask. Nissa had forgotten about the cigarette smoke, and she shouldn't have. It hit her every time. But this winter had been particularly cold and snowy at the North Pole, and the internal heating system at Image Headquarters was very 1950s. It had probably clogged up due to all the tobacco being consumed, and no one had had time in the last few months to do any maintenance.

The pipe and cigar smokers huddled in the back of the conference room, as if they knew they could pollute more air from that location. The cigarette smokers actually tapped their unlit cigarettes on the table, thinking, talking, waiting to light up maybe? They couldn't be grossed out by the cigar smokers, could they?

Everyone around the table was male, again. The older Image Specialists, the men who created the media Santa, were the only ones here. The women who had been working on the tech last time Nissa had come to this conference room were gone.

They were Image Specialists too, but not senior ones. And

Nissa had had their jobs before escaping to the Greater World. They were called "hon," and "sweetie," and were asked to bring coffee, which they did. Nissa had actually talked with personnel more than once, complaining about the atmosphere in Image Headquarters—anonymously, of course—and had been told that Image Headquarters would remain an Old Boys Club until the Old Boys decided to retire.

She had no idea how long that would be, because everyone's lives here were magically lengthened. Even the non-magical humans who came to work here as adults managed to get an extra hundred or so years out of it. Those who had some magic sometimes had two hundred or more years.

And these guys—well, most of them were part elf (some would say part S-Elf, but she didn't really want to look at the genealogies to check)—and she was truly unclear as to how long they lived. Her mother's grandparents still lived, but wouldn't say how old they were. Elves didn't talk about personal things, like longevity or family matters, which was why it took so long for the Image Specialists to come up with an image for Mrs. Claus. She wanted to remain anonymous— and technically she was, since her name was not (in the North Pole, anyway) Mrs. Claus.

In fact, she looked nothing like the rotund, cheerful woman of the Image Specialist's imagination. Nissa always thought of her more as Cruella de Vil—with a mean streak.

But of course Nissa didn't say that. She didn't say much when she was at the Pole. It was safer not to.

And now, she had the meeting she'd been dreading for weeks. In which she would probably have to speak. And, she worried, if she said something wrong, she could lose her job and her beloved New York apartment.

She had worn black pants and a loose red tunic to this meeting, clothes that were easily washed. She actually had started a closet in her mother's house for clothes to wear to

Image Headquarters so that she wouldn't have to destroy her other clothing.

There were no rules to make the Pole more health-conscious, and she had hated that from the beginning. She hated it more now, after indoctrinating herself by watching Ryan's videos.

Maybe he did have a point.

"Ah, Miss Kealoha," said Ludwig, standing and stubbing out his cigar at the same time. "So good of you to join us."

She looked around for Oskar. He leaned against the table in the back, arms crossed. She'd seen that before. He was mad at her, and so he was going to let someone else do the talking.

That the someone else was Ludwig was a bad sign.

"Close the door, please," said Casper, the kindest of the Old Boys. His beard had yellowed from the tobacco he'd smoked over the years, and he actually had a few cigarette burns in it. He'd been such a presence in New York in the 1930s that he had become the inspiration for Seymour Reit and Joe Oriolo, who created Casper the Friendly Ghost. Casper's method of working had always been to pop in, cause some trouble, and pop out, and they recorded that in their original comic.

Nissa leaned out the door, took a deep breath of somewhat-fresh air, and then pulled the door closed, trapping her inside the room with these men—her superiors. Who did not look happy.

She remained standing since they hadn't invited her to sit, both hands on the back of the only available chair.

"Nissa, sweetie," said Sven, one of the Old Boys she never liked to sit near. He had roving hands, although at the moment, they clung to a rather odd-shaped pipe. He was trying to ignite the damn thing—or light it, or whatever anyone called it. He was puffing it, sending out blue smoke to mix with the crud already in the air. "Didn't we tell you to shut down this Professor Palmer?"

She knew it. She knew the Old Boys hadn't liked what happened. She'd played this meeting over and over in her mind. Usually it ended with her being fired. Sometimes, with her in tears. Sometimes with her pounding on the blond wood table and screaming at the Old Boys, telling them what she really thought.

"You did," she said. She felt like she was in a court of law.

"But you didn't do that, did you?" Sven said.

"My understanding," she said slowly, "was that you wanted me to handle him, the way I had handled the previous crisis. In that case, I got reporters to cover the story—"

"And in this case, you agreed with that horrible young man," Ludwig said, his eyes glinting green. Ah, so that was why Oskar wasn't saying anything. They had found her performance awful.

Well, she supposed from their perspective, it was.

She sighed, then wished she hadn't. She had to swallow twice to prevent herself from coughing. "May I tell you what happened from my perspective? Because so much happened behind the scenes."

She sounded formal and proper, the kind of subservient employee they probably wanted to hear from. Or maybe not. Image Specialists were the most unpredictable people in the corporate part of Claus & Company.

They were all staring at her. The pipe smokers had stopped puffing. The cigar smokers had taken their stogies down and were holding them in their hands. The cigarette smokers had never lit up in the first place.

"I'm not sure what you could say," Casper said, his tone kind. "Because we all saw that interview, the one you gave the moment after you returned—"

"Right after we told you to shut him down," Ludwig said.

Her heart was pounding. "You don't know what I could say

because you don't know what happened," she said. "So give me my chance to speak up or fire me now."

She hadn't expected to say that last. She wasn't even sure when the last time someone got fired from the North Pole was. She knew the firing had happened in corporate, but decades ago. Or maybe even a century ago. Before they learned the art of transferring the bad employee to another department, another sector.

Oskar's eyes narrowed. Smoke swirled around him like an aura. He no longer looked like the kindly grandfather type who had spent all his time nurturing her. Now he looked a little like Bad Santa from a thousand bad movies.

No one spoke. No one defended her, and no one mentioned that firing was *not* an option. That was a bit unnerving.

Since no one spoke, she decided to.

"I spoke with Ryan Palmer," she said, deliberately leaving out the fact that the conversation had happened *after* the interview, not before. "He hates the celebrity. He was roped into all that press. He's not going to be around next Christmas. He just wants to teach."

"It doesn't matter," Ludwig said. "He started a conversation. It's continuing. It continued all the way up to the holiday. Some of our staff reported that children at malls were asking Santa to lose weight."

Nissa frowned, not expecting that. She had no idea how the media had handled the Santa story after Palmer left the picture. She'd been working in Last Minute Toys by then.

"You're seeing the children's questions as a bad thing?" she asked, and then knew her response was the wrong one.

Oskar had bent his head down, so that his eyes seemed like slits. He was glaring at her so hard she could feel it from across the room. Maybe he was even using his image magic on her, only in a negative way.

She didn't try to block. She wasn't sure what he was doing,

so she couldn't accurately counteract it. So she decided to ignore him, and speak to the others. They had to understand. Because she might be sacrificing her entire career over this.

"Professor Palmer started a dialogue we *should* be having about revamping Santa's image for the 21st century," she said, her stomach twisting. "After all, you changed his appearance from the 19th to the 20th. The Santa of the post-Civil War newspapers isn't the jolly-faced man of the Coca-Cola ads between the wars."

"Times were bleaker after the war." Sven muttered.

"After which war?" she asked, deciding to stop playing the naïve, subservient employee. "Because times were bleak in the 1930s. Very bleak, in fact, and that's when America's love affair with Santa grew to epic proportions—not in the least because of you, Oskar, and the way you moved with the times."

"You're not going to smooth this over with flattery, missy," Ludwig said, and it looked like he said it before Oskar could get the words out.

Flattery? She hadn't meant that as flattery. She was forming an argument, and they weren't listening.

"I'm not saying this for flattery's sake," she said. "I'm mentioning it because it's been almost a century since we've revamped—"

"We loosened everything in the 1960s," Sven said, tamping on his pipe. "*Everything.* We let others use the brand. We let them make disrespectful films about Santa. Those postcards—"

"Were very creative," she said, trying to get the discussion back on track. She wasn't sure which postcards he was referring to, and she didn't want to know. She didn't want to go into the details. She needed to talk about the overall situation. "But that loosening was more than fifty years ago. Everything we've seen since then was because of the loosening in the 1960s. Nothing new has happened on the Santa Image front since then, and personally, I think that's too long. Change isn't always bad—"

"We know, missy," Ludwig said. "We're the ones who brought change to the Pole in the first place. We're the ones who took our brand out of myth and legend, which varied from country to country, mind you, and decided to homogenize it. We're the ones who saw worldwide potential in a unified message. We're the ones who opened the gates to all of those jobs that exist all over the world because we're the ones who put the name 'Santa Claus' on every lip. We're the ones—"

"But we've skated," Nissa said. They were living so far in the past that she wasn't sure she could bring them out of it. They seemed to hear everything she said as an attack on *them* and not as suggestions for improving Santa's image. They seemed to have no idea at all about the way things were now.

She didn't want them on the defensive. She wanted them to listen to her.

"We're letting others define our brand," she said. "We've let others define Santa since those beer ads from the 1990s. Frankly, I think that a relaxed Santa, sitting on a beach somewhere drinking a beer and staring at the ocean is the wrong direction for our brand. I've always believed that. Why didn't we protest that when it happened? Why isn't anyone mentioning it? Not even Professor Palmer said anything about it."

"Then maybe it's not important," Sven said, fiddling with his pipe.

"Maybe it is. Maybe it's a symptom, and maybe you know it. That's why Professor Ryan bothers you. Because what he's saying is true."

The Old Boys stared at her. She stared back. She was glad they hadn't told her to sit. She actually towered over them, and could look down on them. For a group that specialized in symbolism, they apparently hadn't thought the whole posture thing through. If they had invited her to sit down, she would have had a lot less of their attention.

But she wasn't going to let it go now.

"Why are we so protective of our rum-filled eggnog and Christmas cookies? Are they really that crucial to our brand? Does the Big Guy himself *live* on eggnog and Christmas cookies? I'll wager he's sick of them. He's about so much more than that."

Casper leaned back in his chair and stroked his beard. She couldn't tell, but she had a hunch she had reached him.

"Here's what I don't understand," she said, lowering her voice just a little. "Why aren't we protecting the health of our greatest investment? Why aren't we happy that children want Santa to live longer? Why are we angry at a professor of public health for pointing out something that we should have noticed years ago? Is it *because* we should have noticed it?"

"Those children were just parroting your Professor Palmer," Ludwig said.

"First, he's not 'my' Professor Palmer," Nissa said, even though she wouldn't mind if he were. His image flashed across her mind, and she felt her heart rate increase. Then she forced herself to focus. "Second, children don't 'parrot' professors of public health. Children are actually pretty sensible. Isn't that what you told me when I started at Image Headquarters? That children know what they like and don't like and know more than we give them credit for?"

Ludwig glared at her. Oskar wasn't even looking at her. His head was bowed; he was staring at his shoes as if he were embarrassed for her.

"The children," she continued, "are seeing a problem. They're seeing the same health problems in their schools, in their families. They know that weight is an issue—the entire culture talks about it, and sometimes bluntly, sometimes saying that people who are heavy won't live very long. So why wouldn't children recognize the same in their favorite holiday icon? Why wouldn't they worry?"

"They're not supposed to worry about Santa," Casper said.

"*Exactly*," she said. "And they *are*."

Her words echoed in that crowded room. Casper still stroked his beard. Sven puffed on his pipe, sending small smoke rings into the thick air. Ludwig still glared, and Oskar—Oskar still hadn't looked at her.

Finally he raised his head. Then he stood up—slowly, like a man in pain. His gaze hit hers with such force that it almost hurt.

"The children are worrying," he said, "because you didn't shut down Palmer like we told you to."

Did he just say it was her fault? Was Oskar so egotistical, so *blind*, that he couldn't take criticism?

"Let me get this straight," she said. "You're blaming *me*?"

"For this entire debacle. For Palmer, for the children, for all of it."

They were going to fire her or at least transfer her laterally to some hellhole, like Last Minute Toys. So she might as well speak her mind.

"Really," she said, her voice even softer. But she knew they could hear her in this room. They could probably hear her heartbeat in this room. "So you get rid of me or move me laterally and then what will you do when the next professor of public health or some TV doctor or someone with a vast audience starts complaining about Santa as a role model? Because this is the second time *I've* dealt with it. Sure, Professor Palmer blitzed the US media, but the last guy wasn't American at all. He was Australian, he wrote for a British medical journal, and he got a lot of airplay in the US as well. If those two men, from different parts of the world, come up with this independently of each other, then other people will come to the same conclusion. It won't change. It's happening, and you can't stop it."

"Maybe not now," Oskar said. "You could have stopped it by taking him on one month ago."

She let out a small shocked laugh. "No, I couldn't. You can try to make this my fault, but it has nothing to do with me, and it has everything to do with you."

"Me?" Oskar said, his cheeks fire-engine red—and not in a good way.

"*All* of you," she said. "You all moved here at the same time, and for some reason, you thought you could handle Image Analysis in the Greater World while divorcing yourself *from* the Greater World. You're failing Imagery 101. You know you have to stay in touch with current trends to understand how the masses think—to *manipulate* how the masses think. Instead, you can't even handle a television signal, let alone online chatter. In fact, I'll wager you don't even know what online chatter is. Or how important it is. Or how to access it."

"Now, see here, Missy," Ludwig said.

"Oh, and that?" she said, whirling toward him, pointing a finger in his direction. "That tone, that word 'missy'? It would get you fired in the Greater World, or reprimanded, or at the very least, removed from anything to do with employees. You can't talk to junior executives like that anymore, particularly female execs."

"See?" Sven said in a stage whisper to the Old Boy next to him. "I *told* you this was a feminist thing. They want to overthrow the S-Elf system and install a woman, based on *gender*. *That's* what all of this is about. Forget tradition, forget the way things are, forget all our years of imagery tweaking—"

"And that," Nissa said, putting her hands on the table and bending toward Sven. "That fear of feminists. That's so very 1970s."

They all leaned away from her as if she had thrown something at them. She wondered what that was about. She wished she knew more about internal Pole politics. Because all those rumors about a female S-Elf taking over Santa's role just got a bit more credible.

It also explained some of the animosity coming toward her now.

She was going to take an even bigger risk. She was going to dive straight into something political that she might or might not understand.

"What I'm telling you is a *problem*. It's *not* a feminist thing. It's an out-of-date thing. You're so far behind in everything cultural because none of you have been to the greater World in *decades*. Your junior executives *flee* to the Greater World and we do our best to work within your dictates. But we can't manipulate. We can only maneuver. And it doesn't work."

"You have no right to speak to us that way, *Missy*." It was clear, from the emphasis Ludwig put on the word "Missy" that he was now trying to piss her off.

"I have every right," Nissa said. "Because you're not listening to people on the ground, and you're right: Santa's image has become a crisis. But it's a crisis that you, not that Professor Palmer, made. You're too out of touch to know anything about branding and imaging in this new century, and you're too blind to realize it."

Oskar slammed a fist on the chair beside him. It leapt in astonishment—and she couldn't tell if the leap was because the chair just naturally bounced or if its own internal magic system was startled.

"We were talking about your misbehavior over Palmer," Oskar said, making it sound like she slept with Palmer on national television. If only she *had* slept with him (although not on national television). *Then* she might deserve this treatment. As it stood, Oskar had no right to be this angry with her.

"Really?" she said. "We're talking about Palmer? Because I thought we were talking about Santa's image. Isn't that what this is about? Isn't *that* what we should be focused on here in Image Analysis?"

Oskar's face had turned purple. He opened his mouth to say something else when Casper raised his head.

"It *is* what we should focus on," he said in his calm tone. "And frankly, we haven't been. We've let our most important brand slide. And worse, we've let other people control it."

Nissa felt her breath catch. He was *agreeing* with her?

"Brava, Miss Kealoha. You have somehow gotten it through our—or maybe just my—thick skull that we have not paid the right kind of attention."

"Casper," Oskar said. "You don't understand."

"No," Casper said, and for the first time, Nissa saw the strong man behind the "ghost." "*You* don't understand. Miss Kealoha is right. Palmer is not our problem. We have a much greater one. Palmer is just a symptom."

"Of what?" Ludwig snapped.

"Of our lack of control," Casper said. "Eighty years ago, we would have known about his *book*. We would have seen the threat, maybe before it was published, certainly before his— what is it called? Press tour?—started, and long before he ever showed up on television."

Sven set down his pipe. "We tried to get Miss Kealoha to do her job."

"She *was*," Casper said, "and you don't appreciate it. She's right. We're wrong. And personally, I think she's the one to fix it."

Nissa frowned. She wasn't quite sure what he meant.

"Fix what?" she asked tentatively.

"Everything," Casper said.

CHAPTER 14

RYAN STOOD IN front of the gigantic white board in his favorite classroom. For some reason, his laptop wasn't talking to the projector, and so nothing displayed on the whiteboard at all. All last week, he had compiled a PowerPoint presentation of various public health issues for his 300-level class, Principles of Health Education and Health Promotion.

He had actually looked at his syllabus last week with Nissa in mind, and realized the entire course sounded dull. It wouldn't play on TV and the undergraduates, social media and game junkies all, would consider the coursework too slow.

He thought of developing a health game, like Farmville, but realized he didn't have the time or the know-how. Later, he might talk with the urban planning department. He'd heard that they had successfully used some social media games to show the importance of designing a city correctly. Maybe he could do something similar with the environmental impact on health.

But, he realized, he couldn't do that this semester. All he could do was jazz up the existing material, and that was woefully hard to do. He was well known as one of the best lecturers in the medical school (which the university had folded public health into), but that meant nothing since the level of lecturing expertise in his department was (to be polite) minimal.

So, he'd developed the presentation, and he was proud of it. It actually moved quickly. The music and the images matched and, he realized as he completed it, with some changes, it could be used in health promotion.

One of the wags in his department thought he should add some stuff from his talk show blitz, but even if he could get permissions, he didn't want to. He never wanted to look at himself doing that publicity tour ever again.

Although he wouldn't mind looking at Nissa again. He no longer carried her card with him—he'd weaned himself from it —but he still thought of her way too much.

He hunched over the projector. His first class started in two hours, and if he didn't get the laptop and the projector to talk to each other, he would have to default to the old method of teaching—passing out badly photocopied pieces of paper, and then lecturing about it all. He didn't want to do that.

He had done a lot of soul-searching over the past month. He finally realized that what he wanted to do was what he had thought the book and the book tour would do: teach people how important individual health was to public health. In the last week or so, he'd come to the conclusion that he was better off influencing one student at a time, and giving that student the tools—and the passion!—to proselytize for him. Which meant that he had to step up his game.

Which he wanted to do, if only the damn PowerPoint presentation worked.

He checked the connections, wondered if there was some way to do this all with wireless, and then realized he'd have to rely on the university's wireless network which, in this old concrete bunker, built in the 1970s, barely worked at all.

"Son of a bitch," he muttered, and looked at the whiteboard as if it provided answers. He was going to have to call the university's IT department, and that would tank his entire presentation. IT seemed so proud of the fact that they were *busy*. He always wondered why a university's IT department would be understaffed. Weren't there a million student experts who would work for some kind of credit?

"Problems?" a sexy female voice said behind him. The voice sent shivers through him. It sounded like Nissa, but he had Nissa on the brain so much that he thought half his female students sounded like her. He often found himself peering around corners, thinking he had just gotten a glimpse of her when, indeed, he hadn't seen her at all.

"Computers never work right around me," he said as he continued to fiddle with the laptop. "It's really annoying. Of course, I blame the computers, when in reality, I'm the clueless one. I follow the instructions and still miss somehow..."

He turned around as he said that last, and trailed off when he realized he was looking at Nissa. Or some mental phantom of Nissa. Although he doubted that his imagination was capable of imagining her here, looking like that.

She didn't look at all like the Manhattanite he had seen a month before. She wore appropriate winter attire, for one thing. A heavy, white, parka-like coat over jeans tucked into fur-lined boots that had no heels. She held a pink stocking cap in one hand and mittens in the other. A matching scarf still looped around her neck, making it appear as though her face rested on pinkish snow.

She was even more beautiful than he remembered. Her black hair, mussed a bit on top from the stocking cap, still had a wedge cut, and he couldn't see those pointed ears (if, indeed, he remembered them correctly and hadn't made them up in his fevered [and exhausted] imagination). Her dark eyes twinkled at him. The cold had put so much red in her cheeks that it took him a moment to realize she was barely wearing makeup at all.

"Nissa?" he asked stupidly.

She bowed just a little, and waved her arm in a butlerian flourish. "I'd say 'at your service,' but that implies the wrong things."

And made him imagine the wrong things. He felt the whisper of arousal, but willed it away. He didn't want to think of her that way. (Well, he did, but not right now: not when he had to focus.)

He walked toward her through the maze of metal desk chairs. "I'm..." *honored to see you? Surprised you're here?* Jeez, he didn't even know the right way to talk to her. "I'm...It's..." *great to see you? Fantastic to realize I hadn't imagined you?* "I'm..."

He tripped on one of the chairs, and had to catch himself on the back of the next chair. He was actually happy for the distraction. He was coming off even nerdier than usual.

She grabbed his arm a half second too late, but her grip prevented him from losing his balance. A tingle ran through him. He looked up at her, and when their gazes met, his entire body shivered with pleasure.

"Hi," he said, settling on brevity.

She smiled. "Hi."

"I thought Manhattanites never left the nest," he said, and then wished he hadn't. Had he insulted her? He hadn't meant to. He didn't mean to say anything disparaging about Manhattan, even though the rest of New York hated all the attention it took away from the state.

"Good thing I'm a transplant," she said.

She was? He didn't know that. Of course she was. That indefinable accent.

Her face seemed redder than it had a moment earlier. Maybe the cold hadn't put the roses in her cheeks. Maybe she was embarrassed too. And maybe pigs would fly out of his ass (although he didn't want that to happen; he'd really be embarrassed then).

She finally released his arm. "I came to see you because I need a consult."

"A consult?" He repeated what she said because the speech centers in his brain didn't seem to be working properly. Very little of him (except his hormones) seemed to be working properly. The first time he saw her, he had blamed this reaction on his exhaustion. Now, he was beginning to understand that the problem was just his reaction to her.

"Yeah," she said, but her gaze had moved away from him and settled on the projector. "But it looks like you have a more pressing problem."

"I do?" he asked. *Come on, brain. Get a grip.*

"Do you always have trouble with technology?"

He blinked, once, twice, three times, willing himself to concentrate. "Yes," he said. "It seems to hate me."

"Hmmm," she said, giving him a sideways look that he couldn't really interpret. It was almost as if she were reassessing him. "Any problems on your tour? Cameras giving out? Mics not working?"

"All the time," he said, glad to focus on something else for a moment. "I was beginning to think every single studio had crappy equipment. I know it wasn't me, since I never touched any of it. Usually things go wrong when I touch stuff."

Okay, that sounded stupid too. Because he really wanted to touch her, and he didn't want anything to go wrong.

She didn't seem to notice his discomfort. She didn't even look at him. Instead, she walked toward the projector. She touched it, and he thought he heard something pop.

He said, "I was just about to call the university's IT department—"

"Who is probably sick of you, right?" she asked. And then

she put a hand to her mouth like a child who had misspoken. "I didn't mean that like it sounded."

"Yes, you did," he said with a smile. Maybe he made her nervous too. Or maybe she was one of those people who picked up on other people's nervousness and then got nervous on her own. "And you're right. They *are* sick of me."

"I can get this to work for you," she said. She ran a finger over the laptop, then the projector and then she hit the laptop's space bar. The first image of his PowerPoint presentation showed up on the screen just like it was supposed to.

"How did you do that?" he asked.

She shrugged. "Magic."

"Wish I could replicate that," he said.

"Oh, you probably could," she said. "But no need right now. This should work from now on."

He nodded, wondering how she fixed such a big problem with a simple movement. He had probably missed something obvious. That was usually what happened. And then he felt like an idiot.

Which he did not want to feel like right now—at least about the computer. She wasn't judgmental over it the way that the IT people were. She acted like tech that malfunctioned for no apparent reason was absolutely normal.

He took a deep breath. He was overthinking (and overfeeling) everything. "You said you wanted to consult?"

"I do, but it looks like you have no time." She traced the top of the laptop as she said that, almost as if it had reminded her that he had a real job.

"I have time," he said. "My class doesn't start for another two hours. I'd have to be here, like, in an hour-forty-five, but the point is, that I do have time."

Now the speech centers were overloading him with words. He forcibly shut his mouth so that no more words would emerge.

She smiled, even though the smile didn't quite meet her eyes. "Wonderful," she said—and he wondered why she was no longer as interested as she had seemed just a few moments ago. Had she just remembered what a nerd he could be? Did seeing him in his native environment make him less interesting? (He had no idea how he could be *less* interesting. He'd pretty much hit the rock bottom of interesting the last time she saw him, when he'd been tired enough to fall over in the middle of their conversation.)

"My office is two buildings over," he said, "but there's a small coffee nook upstairs if you don't want to go out in the snow."

"Is it private?" she asked.

The snow? His speech center urged him to ask, but he managed to control that wayward remark. She meant the coffee nook, and he knew that, and a tiny little joke about an unclear antecedent was even nerdier than he wanted to be. He had to tame that weird little voice in his brain somehow, because it was really in overdrive.

"Yeah," he said, "unless there are students in it. Which we won't know until we get there."

"Let's go to your office then," she said. "If you don't mind."

If he didn't mind. He'd been fantasizing about inviting her to his office for weeks now. Only in the fantasies, he'd closed the door, then taken her in his arms, kissed her, and—

Well, none of that would happen here. He knew it. He would just have to convince his overactive imagination of it.

"I don't mind," he said. "I really don't mind at all."

CHAPTER 15

*S*HE SHOULDN'T HAVE come. She realized that when she fixed the projector for him and then told the truth about the way she had done it. *Magic*. What the hell had she been thinking? If he had believed her—and of course he hadn't—then she was revealing secrets (again), and if he hadn't believed her—and of course, he hadn't—then she had just sounded flip, which she had *not* been. She didn't want to seem flip to him, or crazy, or needy, or anything.

If she could have done so in some kind of creative way, she would have fled right then and there, but she couldn't. Instead, she smiled at him, watched as he grabbed his coat from a nearby chair, and then followed him out of the building.

He moved like a runner, with a natural grace that she hadn't expected. He also walked like a man on a mission: she had to hurry to keep up with him.

Instead of focusing on him, she pulled on her mittens, but she slipped her cap into her pocket. She should have worn those ear-warmer things, instead of a cap. Her hair probably looked a mess.

As if that mattered. She wasn't here to seduce him; she was here to talk to him.

Two buildings over sounded far away, but in the vagaries of campus design, it took less time to cross the quad than it did to get out of the building holding his class. He opened a nearly invisible door in the side of a red brick building that looked ancient, and then led her up a flight of well-worn stairs. This building still smelled faintly of chalk and cigarettes, even though she knew that neither had been inside this place for years.

The smell had burrowed into the building's DNA. It had to be one of the oldest buildings on this very old campus.

He pushed open another door, rounded a corner, and waved at a woman sitting at a desk.

"Professor Palmer," the woman started, and then she saw Nissa. The woman smiled, and Nissa knew why. Nissa had spoken to her on the phone not thirty minutes ago. The woman was the department secretary. "You must be Ms. Kealoha."

"I am, thanks. Your directions were good." Nissa spoke as she walked, because Ryan didn't stop. He opened one of three doors in a little alcove and stepped inside a room.

Nissa followed, then stopped as her breath caught. She had been in professors' offices hundreds of times before, and never had she seen anything like this. The windows were large, arched, and mullioned, with a view of the quad she had just crossed. Built-in bookshelves made of something that looked like mahogany covered the remaining walls. The furniture was heavy, old-fashioned, and somehow appropriate.

The desk was in what looked like an antechamber to the rest of the room (which seemed more like a small library than an office), and was the only messy thing around—if you wanted to call stacks of papers messy. Her desk at the office was truly messy—there wasn't a stack to be seen. This was organized, even though there were more papers than she had seen outside of a recycling bin in years.

Ryan glanced at the desk as if contemplating sitting down at it, then walked past it. "Let's sit in here. It's more comfortable."

But he didn't sit down. Instead, he stood near one of the overstuffed leather chairs, and put a hand on its back.

Nissa stopped beside him, uncertain if she should sit in the other overstuffed chair or on the couch, which stood directly across from his chair.

His gaze met hers, and her heart started to beat. Hard. She wanted to kiss him. She really, really wanted to kiss him. Right now. And use the couch for something other than sitting.

It took all of her strength to break that gaze. She wondered if her pupils had dilated; she supposed they had. He had to know how attracted she was to him, right?

She didn't want him to know, because that meant he wasn't attracted. He hadn't acted on it yet.

She walked over to the window and looked at the view, even though it didn't interest her. She had rehearsed this conversation in her head, and she couldn't remember how it was supposed to go.

So she just dove in. "I'm not sure if you remember that I work for Claus & Company."

"I do," he said. He sounded different here. Calmer. More relaxed. Maybe that computer thing had really upset him.

"I—um—I got into a lot of trouble for agreeing with you last month."

"I'm sorry," he said, as if it were his fault.

She turned. He was still holding that chair. In fact, the chair was between them like a shield. So he wasn't attracted, and he had noticed her interest. He didn't want her near him.

Her heart sank.

"It's not your fault. You have a good argument."

He shook his head, and she could tell he was going to reiterate that it wasn't his main argument. She didn't need to hear that.

Before he could speak, she said, "I finally convinced my bosses that they were the ones who were out of touch. But now, they expect me to start crafting Santa's 21st century image. What they want is to keep it exactly the same, only make it different, and I want it to reflect current society, and be good for children. I know you're not a professor of marketing or anything, but you have some really good ideas, and I think you're right about the importance of brands and role models in the health arena and...."

She let her voice trail off. He was just staring at her, as if she had lost her mind. Maybe she had. She could do this without him. They both knew that. She *should* do this without him, because Santa's image wasn't really about marketing or branding, but about keeping him relevant in the 21st century, maybe even a force for good. And no professor of public health, no matter how sexy and charismatic, could help her with that.

So she shrugged and decided to go for broke. He was already looking at her like she was crazy; how could telling the truth make that worse?

"And, honestly," she said, "I just wanted to see you again."

He swallowed visibly. "You're kidding," he said, and then looked appalled that those words had come out of his mouth.

"No," she said. "I'm not kidding. I—um—I haven't been able to stop thinking of you since that day in the studio. I've never quite met anyone like you before."

He let out a small laugh. "I'm not sure that's a compliment."

"It's not meant as one. It's the truth. I find you—" she decided to go for broke. "—fascinating. I find you fascinating."

And charming and handsome and funny and appealing and oh, so, sexy. She wanted to tell him all that, but felt like she had revealed too much with "fascinating."

His fingers clutched the top of the chair so hard that his knuckles had turned white. "I'm awake, right?"

"What?" she asked, not sure she understood him.

"This isn't a dream, is it?" Then he shook his head and rolled his eyes just a little. "Of course, even if it is, you wouldn't tell me. People in dreams don't know they're dreaming."

"What?" she asked again.

"I'm—ah, hell." He stepped around the chair and walked toward her. Her heart pounded. Then he put his hands on her shoulders for just a moment, standing so close to her that she could feel the heat from his body.

His gaze held hers—that magnetic gaze—and then, then, he leaned toward her slowly. He was going to kiss her or maybe he was asking permission to kiss her or maybe—

She didn't care. She slipped her arms around his waist and pulled him close. Then she kissed him.

He tasted of sunshine mixed with just a hint of chocolate and mint. She pressed against him, felt more muscles than she had expected (public health, right? That included exercise, right?) and then melted into him.

His hand slipped from her shoulders, up her neck, cupping her chin, then getting tangled in her hair. His touch was gentle and erotic at the same time. His thumbs found the slightly pointed edges of her ears—that legacy from her mother that she had always hated—and he moaned slightly.

His kiss got more passionate, his body even closer, despite all their winter clothes. She started to slip her hands under his sweater when he suddenly broke away from her.

"I—I—I—have a class," he said. His cheeks were flushed, his eyes bright, and his lips just a little swollen. "I'm sorry. If I didn't stop, well, I wouldn't have stopped. I mean, I think you're the most gorgeous woman I've ever seen, and I'm such an idiot, I probably just ruined everything, and I want nothing more than to—"

She leaned into him, kissing him again, slipping her hands under his sweater anyway, feeling how warm his skin was. She could kiss him forever, classes be damned, but she had control too, just not as much of it as she had initially thought because this kiss was going on longer than she had originally intended and she wanted nothing more than to make him miss that class, but then he might resent her or someone might knock on the door or—

She made herself break off the kiss. She was breathing as hard as if she had just snowshoed fifteen miles.

"I—you're right," she said. "You need to go to your class. But I would love to take you to dinner. I'd say it was to pick your brain, but really, I just want to—"

"I know," he said and kissed her yet again. She had been about to say *get to know you better*, but this was good, this was better than good, this was *great* in fact and perfect and her hands were reaching, not for his sweater this time, but for the edges of his pants, and she made herself stand back, even though that meant ending what she considered to be the best kiss of the three.

"Dinner?" she asked again. "Is there somewhere good around here?"

He stared at her for a long moment, as if he wasn't sure what she was asking. Finally, he said, "You are the most beautiful woman I have ever seen."

She smiled, because she didn't know what else to do. Her mother had once told her that she should never deny a compliment, but she wanted to. She also wanted to reach out and grab him again, so she took another step backwards, just so that she wouldn't get lost in another kiss.

"Your class," she said as a reminder.

"Yeah, right, of course," he said. "And dinner. God. Dinner. How about—oh, God, you're used to Manhattan. There's nothing good here."

"Then let's go somewhere bad," she said.

His eyes twinkled, and she realized exactly how he had taken that. She wasn't going to correct him. If he wanted to go somewhere bad with her, then she was willing.

"There's Frank's Country Restaurant," he said after a moment. "Around here, we call it carbo-loaders paradise."

"So, not a place a professor of public health should be seen," she said.

"We public health professors are not subject to those rules," he said, "so long as the place passes its health inspections."

"And has it?" she asked.

"Oh, yeah." His gaze had never left hers. If she moved even slightly, they'd be in each other's arms again. "It's the best worst place in town."

"Sounds perfect," she said.

"Yeah," he said. "I guess it does."

CHAPTER 16

*I*F HE WERE a smarter man, he would have cancelled class and just made love to her on that couch, all day long, uncurtained windows be damned. His entire job be damned. He would have sacrificed it all for her.

If he were a smarter man.

But he didn't think of that option until he started the PowerPoint presentation, after the lights had dimmed in class, as the presentation ran more or less on its own, and he had to stay turned slightly away from the class because every time he thought of her, his body reacted in ways he didn't want his students to see.

But it was more than just lust. He'd been in lust before, and he'd always known that once it was slaked, he would be able to walk away. This was something else. Something about this woman called to him from deep within, as if he had met a missing piece of himself, which was so stupid, because unless people truly were missing pieces of themselves (from accidents or whatever) they were always whole. Or so he had told one of his girlfriends once when she said that everyone had the perfect soul mate somewhere, the person who completed them, and he wasn't that person for her.

You're being unrealistic, he'd said, even though he hadn't wanted her to stick around. He had almost told her that those high standards would make her end up alone and unwanted, but he'd stopped himself, because he recognized in that last moment just how cruel he would sound.

But those words had never left him: the lack of realism in that longing for the "perfect" mate.

Whom he had just found.

And if he told Nissa that, she'd run from him, he knew it. *He* would run from him if he had said that and he were her, or something like that.

His thoughts had been tangled since those kisses, and he wasn't sure he would ever have clarity back. He wasn't even sure how he made it through his class.

Or the next one.

Or how he had prevented himself from running down the slippery sidewalk to the faculty parking lot.

Or how he managed to drive to Frank's Country Restaurant and how he managed not to be too early, but early enough to get a table, even though it was the dinner rush.

For sixty years, Frank's Country Restaurant had done its best to bring the country into Upstate. In the middle of delis, diners, and bad Italian restaurants, Frank's had once been an oasis of middle-American blandness. Now, though, it was a nostalgic place in the midst of vegan restaurants and upscale boutique restaurants so expensive that Ryan was afraid he'd pay more for a meal than he did for his mortgage payment.

Frank's had become the go-to place for him, and for everyone else in town on a real-world salary. This evening, though, he saw it through Nissa's Manhattan eyes, and realized he probably should have taken her to one of the upscale boutique restaurants.

The décor was shabby, the booths a bit tattered, the windows clean but scratched. No one had updated the carpet since the 1990s. There was a real jukebox in the corner that only played four songs, because the company that ran it had gone out of business years ago.

Families crowded the tables, children screamed on their way to the designated play area, and the salad bar looked like a bomb had gone off in the middle of it. (The bomb was probably a small group of ten-year-olds who were currently throwing cherry tomatoes at each other in the play area.)

Ryan let out a small sigh and wished he had gotten Nissa's cell phone number. He also wished he had her card. Maybe the number on that would take him directly to her. Only he had deliberately tried not to memorize the number. He hadn't wanted to dial her late one night when his resistance was down.

"Hey, Prof!" Henry Hewitt, one of his best students, waved at him from the cash register. "You meeting that gorgeous woman from the talk show?"

Ryan felt like he'd been outed in more ways than one: first, he hadn't realized anyone in town had seen those talk shows since no one talked to him about them, and second, he hadn't expected anyone to recognize Nissa. The fact that Henry *had* recognized Nissa meant she had beaten him to the restaurant. Ryan couldn't back out now.

"Yeah, I am," Ryan said, unable to find a better way to answer that question. "She's here, huh?"

"In back," Henry said. Then he grinned and said softly, "Nice goin', Dude."

Thanking Henry for that comment felt inappropriate, so Ryan just nodded his acknowledgement and walked to the part of the restaurant that locals considered the back. It was techni-cally the side of the restaurant—the back was where the play area was—but it felt farther back than the play area. In class, he'd once used that discrepancy as an example of the way that perception influenced fact.

Nissa sat alone at one of ten tables. It seemed amazingly quiet here, especially in comparison to the rest of the restaurant. She had already ordered something to drink; he smelled Frank's winter specialty hot chocolate, made with a touch of mint.

As he sat down, Ryan said, "If I'd realized what a zoo this place would be tonight, I would have picked somewhere else."

"I like it," Nissa said. "You don't see a lot of places like this in my neighborhood."

She was right; Manhattan wasn't known for its kid-friendly restaurants except in touristy Times Square.

Ryan smiled as one of the waitresses came over. She too was a student, but not from his classes. He just recognized her from campus.

He ordered some coffee and took the offered menu. So did Nissa. But neither of them looked at it. Instead, they stared at each other.

He wondered if she regretted all those kisses this afternoon, then decided he had to stop worrying about her. She had confessed that she had come to see him, which surprised him. He had felt as if he'd been at his very worst every time she'd seen him.

"How did class go?" she asked, apparently not realize he had taught two since he last saw her.

"Better than I expected, which isn't saying much. My PowerPoint presentation would have been a real disaster if it weren't for you."

She shrugged. "Nothing to it."

"It was to me," he said. "Thank you."

"You're welcome." They stared at each other for a moment and he could feel the attraction thrumming between them.

"It's cliché," he said, "but I really don't know much about you. You said you weren't a native New Yorker...?"

It was a better conversational gambit than the ones he'd tried this afternoon. And better than asking her how she got her start with Claus & Company, which he had looked up on the internet one late night while he was staring at her card. Like most corporate websites, the Claus & Company site had told him next to nothing about the company, but unlike the others, he couldn't drill down into the site to learn stuff the company didn't want him to know.

"I thought you could tell from my accent," she said. "It was pretty bad when I moved here."

"From where?" he asked.

She looked down, which surprised him. She also started to answer and stopped herself, which surprised him more. It was almost as if she had edited her response.

"I was born in Hawaii," she said, "but I was raised in a place no one's ever heard of."

"Try me," he said.

She frowned just a little, as if she were measuring her response. Then she said something that sounded like the combination of a cough, a sneeze, and someone clearing their throat.

"Excuse me?" he said.

She repeated the noise—which was apparently a name, or a word or something. "At least," she added, "that's what we call it."

And then she looked down again, as if she were embarrassed to admit she came from that place.

"What do we call it?" he asked.

She bit her lower lip. Then she closed her eyes. Finally she put a hand over her mouth, as if she were holding back words.

The entire situation had suddenly become weird.

"Nissa?" he asked.

"The North Pole," she said after a moment. "You call it the North Pole."

CHAPTER 17

S HE COULDN'T LOOK at him as she said it, but she couldn't lie to him either. The lies simply wouldn't come out of her mouth. Twisting the truth only worked part way.

Her magic was clashing with his somehow, and it was creating an honesty that she wasn't used to, particularly since she was in advertising, promotion, and marketing.

Or maybe, she was just so attracted to him her entire being rebelled when she tried to lie.

"Nice try," he said. "Now, tell me where you're really from."

She raised her head. She was miserable. She actually wanted to spend more time with him and she now knew that was impossible.

"I'm from the North Pole," she said.

"Yeah, right," he said with a laugh. "Next thing you know, you'll tell me you're an elf."

"Half," she said.

He grinned, then the grin slowly faded. "Half?"

"On my mother's side." Her voice was flat. "My father's mostly native Hawaiian."

Ryan opened his mouth, then closed it. "How does that happen?" he blurted.

"Vacation," she said, because the only other options were to explain to him how the birds and bees worked or the way that elves and humans really were sexually compatible, despite what the literature said.

"Vacation?" he asked, mimicking her tone.

She nodded, her throat constricting. She managed to say, "People take them, you know. Even elves. Usually in January."

"Oh," he said, clearly confused by this conversation. "So you're on vacation?"

"I should be," she said, feeling miserable. "Because this was a mistake."

She pushed away from the table, rattling her hot chocolate mug. She shouldn't have been honest—not that she had a choice—and she shouldn't have pursued him—and there she *had* had a choice—and she should have just talked to him about Claus & Company and branding.

She took a ten from her wallet and put it on the table, even though that was more than her hot chocolate cost by a long ways.

"I'm sorry," she said, and walked away.

CHAPTER 18

SHE WAS LEAVING. Ryan stood up, not sure exactly what had happened, and hurried after her. He joined her in the main room, caught her by the arm, and said, "What just happened?"

"Nothing," she said, shaking her head. "You wouldn't believe it, no matter what I said."

"Make me believe," he said.

She stopped in the middle of all the misbehaving children, and looked at them as if they held the secret to life.

"That's the thing," she said. "I can't make anyone believe anything. It's against the rules."

And she shook him off.

This time, he couldn't catch up with her. By the time he reached the front door, she had vanished. He didn't even see a car pulling out of the parking lot.

He stood in the cold for a long moment, staring into the darkness.

The parking lot was empty; the road was empty. Even the cross streets were empty. It was as if she had never existed.

He had no idea what had happened. He hadn't said anything

wrong, that he knew of. He'd asked her about her life, and she'd told him about...the North Pole?

Was she crazy?

Was he?

Because part of him did believe her. She had pointed ears. He'd seen them. Her business card never tattered, despite how he held it. She always talked about branding Santa, as if she were in control of that.

Santa couldn't be real. Because Ryan's Uncle Dave had played Santa at every Christmas party since Ryan could remember. His Uncle Dave, who was a bit too fat, whose ears were round and whose cheeks were rosy—not from cold, but from broken capillaries, just like his nose was too red. Uncle Dave, whom everyone struggled to keep sober until his time with the kids was over.

"Professor Palmer?" Henry peered out the door. "You gonna order?"

What did Ryan say about this? That his date had run off? That she was half-elf? That she was crazy?

That he thought maybe he was in love with her anyway? That the tips of those ears turned him on like nothing else ever had in his entire life?

"Yeah," Ryan said after a moment. "Yeah, I guess I will order. Just give me a minute, okay?"

"Okay," Henry said, and closed the door.

Ryan stood outside a moment longer, his arms wrapped around himself, shivering, watching his breath fog in and out.

Christmas. The North Pole, Claus & Company, Santa in the 21st century. Elves.

He should have been appalled—and he *was*—but for the wrong reason.

He should have stopped her.

Instead, he had let her walk away.

CHAPTER 19

*D*UMB. THAT'S WHAT she was. Dumb. She'd dated guys in the Greater World before, and she'd lied to them the whole time. If she accidentally used magic, she said it was luck or just something weird or, worse, she'd tell them they hadn't seen what they had just seen.

She had pretty much kept to herself, though, because the strain of keeping the lies straight was always a tad too hard. And she didn't want to date any of the men—human, elven, or a mixture—at the Pole because long-distance relationships didn't work.

And, to be honest, everyone in the Pole (and some of the Claus & Company people outside of it) had a pretty insular view of the world. All the worlds—the Greater World and the magical world.

She had actually used magic to get to her car. She'd propelled herself there, rather like flying but not quite, because she couldn't quite manage that. More like running super fast—something every child learned and something she hadn't done in years. Then she had cloaked the car in an invisibility spell.

She hadn't driven away. She just sat inside the car, watching

Ryan as he stood in the door to the restaurant, looking at the parking lot, then scanning the roads. Was he hoping to see her? Maybe. Maybe he thought it was all a joke.

Maybe he thought she'd apologize, or maybe he'd lie to her and say that he *did* believe, when clearly he didn't. Santa was a fictional character to him, an advertising creation, an *example* in Ryan's long book on the importance of the individual in public health.

She shouldn't have come here. She shouldn't have tried to talk to him. She should have stayed in Manhattan and let that one day in December remain one of her most special memories. One she could watch over and over again in digital download, just to see his handsome face.

Which continued to scan the parking lot as if he knew she were there.

Finally, one of the wait staff peered out the door, talked to him for a moment, and then went inside. Ryan nodded, gave the parking lot one last look, and followed the young man through the door.

It was over.

Maybe the Old Boys were right: maybe she had mishandled all of this because of her attraction to Ryan. Not that the Old Boys knew about the attraction; they hadn't, and they hadn't accused her of it.

But they had thought her judgment was clouded, and they might have been right.

Santa was her responsibility. Updating the Greater World New York office was her new task.

She was supposed to think about the future of Claus & Company, not about her relationship with a professor named Ryan Palmer.

Who kissed like no one she had ever met.

Who attracted her like no one she had ever known.

Who would be impossible to forget.

CHAPTER 20

*T*WENTY-FOUR HOURS LATER, Ryan still didn't understand what had happened, and that bothered him. Because he was a logical man who could generally figure out most things, given enough time.

He'd gone to his office at four A.M. when he couldn't sleep, and except for leaving once to teach a two-hour lab, he had spent the entire time on his computer, reading about the historical Santa Claus.

If, indeed, anyone could call Santa historical.

But, he supposed, people could label Santa historical. Because the creation of the beloved children's character could be traced. There was a trail, which began with the myths and legends of all the Northern European countries. They all had different names for him, like Father Christmas and St. Nicholas. But there were parts in all of those creations in the modern American Santa Claus.

That Santa seemed to appear first in the American Civil War. By the beginning of the 20th century, Santa was used to sell things, including—one could argue—Christmas itself. Selling things made sense, because advertising really picked up at the turn of the last century—in newspapers, magazines, and other things.

Ryan had actually done research into the rise of mass media and its impact on public health. Public health advocates hadn't used mass media properly except in cases of severe contagion or a short-term threat to a community.

Before the debacle of the last book and the stupid book tour, he'd actually been thinking his *next* book would be about ways to use media to change images of health. Those thoughts had led to the Santa chapter. He had considered it a toe into the realm of media and health.

He hadn't expected to get burned.

He wasn't sure he would ever write another book. Wendy had told him that he was a celebrity now, and his work would get scrutinized. She had also told him that she would represent him through the university, and he would be able to get on any show he wanted. The president of the university seconded that, wanting the press for the school.

Ryan didn't want to do any of it. Just thinking about Santa brought it all back.

But he forced himself, because if he didn't, he might not ever see Nissa again. He wanted to see her. Even if she was crazy.

Health. He had to focus on health, including his. The very idea of losing Nissa had taken him out of his comfort zone, and he found that crazy all by itself.

Because he had never had her. He had met her twice and been somewhat obsessed with her. He had used the memory of her to get himself through a difficult experience, and that had forced him to focus on her.

That was all.

He rubbed his hand over his eyes. They ached from lack of sleep and because of the research he'd done, with the lights down and squinting at his computer.

He wouldn't have done the research if he were merely focused on her. He'd found other women stunningly beautiful or intellectually intriguing. He'd thought about them a lot, but when he was with them, he never felt like he had just been with the one person he'd spent his whole life waiting for.

And if he tried to apply his logical brain to that thought, his logical brain sent all kinds of warning signals to the rest of him. Because he had never ever believed in soul mates or in true love or in love at first sight. He believed in long-term friendships and relationships that grew and became something else.

Even though he'd never really experienced those either.

He stood up, stretched, and heard his back crack. He'd clearly been sitting here too long, researching and not processing the information.

He had been trying to figure out more than just Santa. He'd been trying to figure out what was going on in his own head. Or, to be more accurate, in his own heart.

And maybe internet research was the wrong approach.

What if he had misunderstood her? Was she an "elf" as in an employee of this company called Claus & Company which (somewhat secretly) controlled Santa's brand?

She hadn't said anything about magic. Maybe she had been making a joke about being half-elven—or elfish? Jeez, he didn't even know what a group of elves were called. (And why would he? He was a *scientist,* not an elf expert.)

Nissa hadn't said that she knew a man who could fly all over the world in one night, deliver toys to only the best children (ignoring all the poor ones), and somehow still remain a hero.

She didn't seem delusional. The studios in New York didn't treat her that way.

The studios in New York didn't think so. In fact, the

producers on Becker's show had called her a go-to guest. So someone had vetted her, right?

She had seemed sane. She *was* sane. Although her reaction after telling him she was from the North Pole had been weird. Had she seen the perplexed look on his face? Had he made some kind of judgmental expression, something that a sensitive woman who had just put herself on the line would run from?

Why had she run from him? She had called their dinner—or her trip to the university—a mistake. A *mistake*.

Clearly he had done something wrong.

He shoved his hands in the back pockets of his jeans and walked to the windows. The safety lamps, installed every 15 feet, sent a warm, yellow glow along the paths, making the campus look like something out of an early 20th century idyll. A few students walked by, their shapes indistinct because of the frozen moisture in the air.

He had been the problem, not her. He had gone up to her and asked her to help him believe. Maybe they had spoken at cross-purposes. He had asked her what happened, and she had responded: *You wouldn't believe it, no matter what I said.*

Believe what? He had assumed she was talking about Santa, when she might have been talking about his expression or the fact that she hated the food in the restaurant or maybe that she had never dated. He hadn't asked for clarification.

Instead, stupidly, he had assumed that she had been talking about Santa Claus. *Santa Claus*. Whose name hadn't even come up in the conversation.

In fact, he believed that the conversation had been about Santa so much that he had spent the last ten hours researching the "historical" man, not thinking about Nissa.

Thinking about Santa.

Ryan leaned his head against the window's cool glass. He had asked Nissa to "make him believe." And even that question had been wrong.

Because he clearly believed. He believed so deep down that he thought there was a possibility that she worked for Santa—or that she thought she worked for Santa. And then Ryan had blamed her for being crazy or delusional, when that very assumption was just crazy or delusional.

Whatever had given him the idea that she was a "real" elf? Or a "real" half-elf. Her pointed ears? A lot of perfectly normal humans had pointed ears. And hers weren't even that pointed. They just had a nifty little tip to them that, even as he thought of it, still turned him on.

He groaned.

He had been the idiot, not her. He had made some kind of face, he had maybe not understood a joke, he had taken everything too seriously, just like he always had, and she had fled from him.

She had fled.

He lifted his head, his forehead still chilled from the window.

For the entire time he'd known her, he'd been exhausted, overwhelmed, and out of his depth. Even his brother had noted at Christmas that Ryan hadn't seemed like himself.

Teaching didn't bring him the joy it had years ago, and even standing here made him uncomfortable.

Ryan had been off and his reactions had been off and he had probably offended Nissa without even realizing it.

He owed her an apology.

He had her business card on his desk. He could call her.

And she could hang up on him.

Or he could go to Manhattan and drop in at her office, maybe buy her lunch, maybe try again.

She would probably say no to that, but at least they would have one last opportunity.

At least, he would get to see her one last time.

$\mathcal{T}$HE OFFICES OF Claus & Company were on Madison Avenue in a building the company had owned since the 1920s. Claus & Company was its own corporation, but it also owned a major advertising company—one that Oskar had started in the 1940s. That company still existed, and it was still very, very important in the US advertising business, but it had little to do with Nissa's work.

Until today. She had scheduled an appointment to talk with their president, their top-earning adman, and the most up-and-coming person in the firm, whoever that might be.

The meeting had gone pretty well. She had brought in a list of questions from the most basic to some very complex ones. She knew better than to change a brand immediately—Coke had famously made that mistake in the 1980s, and it was still the poster-child for what not to do—but she also knew they had to slide Santa's image into the 21st century.

She wanted a proposal from the ad firm, and they promised her one. She also knew that the moment she had left the president's office, he had called Oskar to see if she was authorized to do this.

She tried to pretend it didn't bother her.

She was trying to pretend that a lot of things didn't bother her. She was trying to pretend that nothing bothered her, particularly that ill-advised drive two days ago to see Ryan.

Professor Palmer. She wasn't going to call him Ryan any more. That implied a familiarity she didn't want to think about, just like she didn't want to think about those kisses. Just like she didn't want to think about the look on his face when she got up from the table, or the way he had peered into the parking lot when she was hiding from him.

She had felt ridiculous in that moment: it had taken all of her strength not to go back and apologize.

And then what? Even more ridicule, this time from him, as she told him about magic and how the system worked to make sure there were enough toys, how Claus & Company was working to make sure children didn't fall through the cracks.

She couldn't explain her life any more than he—or anyone from the Greater World—could understand it.

She took the elevator to her office. This old building had been remodeled so many times in her short tenure that she was always surprised to see the wall of mirrors, the dark wood paneling, and the fancy buttons on the elevator itself. In her mind, it was still a 1970s box that shuddered as it moved.

Everything had changed in the years since she'd started working here, and she used to accept that as part of life in this building. Now, she saw it as a passage of time. She'd been here long enough to see three iterations of the *elevator* design, for heaven's sake, and only now was she getting enough clout to actually do something about Santa's image.

Even though the clout wasn't that great; not if the president of the ad agency below was calling Oskar to see if Nissa actually had the authority to hire the agency to present a few ideas.

She decided she wasn't going to focus on any of it any more.

She had some ideas on her tablet, ideas she hadn't told the ad guys about because she wanted to come up with her own campaign. She would develop the best thing for her company, all on her own. She still had to present it to Oskar and the Old Boys anyway; it would be best if the ideas that got so horribly shot down (and all her ideas would get shot down; she just knew it) would be hers, so she didn't have to blame someone else.

Maybe then she would quit, permanently move to New York, and get some fluffy show on her favorite network, talking about advertising and media relations or about holidays or images or something she could convince them she was qualified to talk about for one hour once a week.

She was so engrossed in her work that she barely noticed her secretary clear his throat as she walked by. Fyodor rarely did that, even when he was ill, so she took two more steps before the sound actually registered.

She raised her head and saw—

Ryan, sitting on the red-and-white striped candy-cane couch that had been in the office since the dawn of time. He stood as his gaze met hers.

Fyodor, who had escaped the Pole as soon as he graduated from secondary school and who was using this job to fund his way through NYU to get a degree in theater, raised his eyebrows. His lips were twisted in a slight smile, as if the entire situation amused him.

Which it probably did. He had been one of the people who had urged her to go Upstate, just to see where she stood, and then had been disappointed when she returned, unwilling to talk.

To talk. About Ryan. Who was standing here, looking very uncertain. And very handsome in a pair of tight blue jeans and a black sweater that accented his broad shoulders and dark hair.

"Hi," he said, sounding uncertain. "I thought maybe I owed you an apology."

"You didn't do anything," she said. "I was the one who ran out on you."

Fyodor's eyebrows rose even higher, something Nissa hadn't thought possible.

She gave him a withering glance, not that it would make a difference. He would react as long as she and Ryan stood in the reception area.

"Why don't you come into my office?" she asked, even though she really didn't want him to. She didn't want to explain herself, she didn't want to humiliate herself, she didn't want to think about that evening any more.

Even though she couldn't really stop thinking about it.

Without waiting for Ryan's answer, she pushed open the office door and stepped inside. Like everything at Claus & Company, her office smelled faintly of peppermint and evergreen. She only noticed the scent when someone else sniffed the air and looked both surprised and pleased.

Her office was large for Manhattan—a corner suite that had once belonged to Oskar, it was larger than most apartments. She had a couch, a large desk in one corner, and her computer desk in another. Her view wasn't as impressive—she got to see the street and nearby buildings—but it was better than no view at all.

Ryan closed the door behind him, and her heart started to race. The last time she had been alone with him in an office, she had kissed him silly.

This time, she put Oskar's old desk between herself and Ryan.

"Have a seat," she said, hoping she sounded calmer than she felt.

Ryan looked at the chair in front of the desk as if it would trap him. "I don't plan to stay long enough," he said. "I just wanted to say I was sorry. I enjoyed our time together, and I know that something went wrong, and it was probably me—"

"It wasn't you," she said. That honesty, leaping out of her. She should have agreed with him. She should have blown him off. They weren't suited, and he didn't even know why. She didn't want to tell him why, either, because then he'd either think her a lunatic, or she would violate the rules of the North Pole and Claus & Company. She didn't like either choice.

"I don't pretend to understand what happened," he said, looking at that chair again. "But I do know I wasn't at my best in either of our encounters. I find you fascinating, Nissa, and I'd love to get to know you better—"

"That's the point," she said. "You can't."

He let out a slow breath. "Because you're already involved with someone?"

He sounded hopeful, as if that were the problem instead of her weird behavior in the restaurant.

"Because of this job," she said, and hoped it would be enough.

"I understand when someone has to work long hours," he said.

She shook her head. "Please, Ryan," she said. "I'm not sure I can explain this in a way that will satisfy both of us."

That, at least, was true.

He frowned. For a moment, she thought he was going to turn around and leave. Then he sighed, pulled the chair back, and sat down heavily.

"Give it a try," he said.

She closed her eyes. If only he would leave. But part of her was happy he was staying, happy that he wasn't going to take no for an answer, happy—that he'd end up thinking ill of her?

She opened her eyes. "Would you like some hot cocoa?" It was the only gambit she had.

"No," he said. "I just want to talk."

"Coffee, then," she said.

"No," he said. "Please, just—"

"I think you should have coffee," she said, and waved her right hand. Little sparkles—almost like glitter—covered the air around her. Then a red-and-green Santa mug filled with coffee appeared on the desk in front of Ryan.

"How did you do that?" he asked.

She wasn't going to tell him, not yet, despite the fact that the word *magic* just about tripped off her tongue. She kept the word back and instead said, "Do you take cream or sugar?"

He peered into the mug. The coffee was black and rich; the best she could think of. "Soy milk," he said almost absently.

She waved her hand again, and the glitter reappeared. He was still looking at the mug. She could see the liquid from her perch on the edge of her chair. The coffee was a milk-chocolate color now.

"Too much?" she asked. "Too little?"

"Just right," he said in a small Baby-Bear voice. But he didn't pick up the mug. "You didn't answer me. How did you do that?"

This time the word fell out of her mouth. "Magic."

He looked up at her. That jolt when his gaze met hers, it never disappointed. It always made her feel special, even now, even when it was clear he was perturbed.

"Is that your usual answer when you don't want to explain something?" he asked. "You said the same thing about the projector."

The projector and his comments that day reminded her of something. "You told me that you always have trouble with technology," she said.

"Don't change the subject," he said.

"I'm not," she said. "Just bear with me. Technology. It fritzes around you, doesn't it? I noticed you don't keep your computer on your main desk. Neither do I."

She indicated the computer desk across the room.

"Still," she said, "I go through a computer every 18 months. So does everyone else in this office."

"Get your electrical system checked," he said, sounding annoyed.

"It's not the electrical system," she said. "The advertising agency downstairs doesn't have this problem. Neither does the modeling agency upstairs. Just us."

He sighed. "Why is this relevant?"

"Because," she said, "you told me that the studios you went to always had equipment failure, but you knew it couldn't be about you. Yet, if you were to call the studio where we met and ask them how many times equipment failed around me, you know what they'd say?"

"Stop wasting our time?" he asked.

"Every fourth visit," she said, ignoring his tone. "It's a standing joke with us. They think it's the luck of the draw. It's not."

His shoulders slumped. "You're not one of those people who claims to have some kind of weird energy that destroys electronics, are you? Someone who says watches don't run around them."

"They don't run on you, do they?" Nissa asked, taking a gamble. He wasn't wearing a watch. "You always blame it on lack of care or the fact that you buy cheap watches, but you stopped wearing them, what, when you were twelve? Thirteen?"

His gaze narrowed. She was right; she could tell from his expression. "Why is this important?" he asked.

She snapped her fingers and the mug of coffee disappeared.

"I'd be more impressed if this were my office," he said. "Then I'd know the desk wasn't rigged, and I would know you hadn't performed some kind of parlor trick."

"Hold your hand out flat," she said.

He gave her a weird look, then did it. She snapped her

fingers a second time, and the coffee mug reappeared balanced on his palm, a candy cane stirring stick in the center of it.

"You've gotta be kidding me," he said.

"Magic," she said again.

He stared at the coffee. The mug had to be burning his palm. He took his left hand and grabbed the mug's handle, then took a sip. The candy cane stir-stick hit him in the nose. He frowned.

"I have two questions," he said after he finished swallowing. "Do you really believe you work for the 'real' Santa Claus, and what does my lack of a watch have to do with anything?"

She wanted to answer the second question first. It was the easier question. Kinda. Sorta. But she knew better than to do that. The first question was the one that would guarantee whether or not he would stay in the room. The second question might just remain permanently unanswered.

She sighed. "I work for the real Santa Claus."

He let out a small snort and shook his head. But he didn't move. "A guy who flies around the world one night a year, gives toys only to 'deserving' kids, and then crawls back in his ice cave."

"No," she said. "That guy doesn't exist."

Ryan frowned, then took another sip of his coffee. He ran a finger along the edge of her desk where the mug had first appeared, apparently felt nothing, and then set the mug in that spot.

She was tempted to make it disappear again, but she didn't.

"So you work for...a company that 'owns' Santa's brand? And they call all the people who work for that company 'elves'?" His emphasis on the two words was so strong, she almost expected him to make air quotes with his fingers.

"No," she said. "I work for Claus & Company. We've been around for centuries, and we are run by someone that the world calls Santa Claus. We mostly focus on charitable works, but the toy-giveaway has been part of our focus for centuries. We can't do that with everyone, so we give children of other traditions what we can. That's really not my area. I handle public relations in the United States—"

"Public relations," he said. "For a man who flies around the world in one night. Which is physically impossible."

"Yeah, it would be," she said. "If it weren't for magic."

He nodded. This was the telling moment, the moment when he should walk away. "And you're magical."

"You are too," she blurted.

"Now you're going to tell me that every kid has magic," he said, "and then we're going to sing a happy tune."

She smiled in spite of herself. "No," she said. "Not everyone has magic. But you have a lot, which shows up as charisma and charm. Your family is also extremely long-lived, and I would wager that they immigrated from a middle-European country that either no longer exists or from an area no genealogist can track down exactly."

He leaned back a little. She was spot-on, she knew it. "You researched my family?"

"No," she said. "I just know a Charming when I meet one."

"A Charming," he said.

She didn't want to explain how all the magic systems were related, from elves to fairies to fairy tales to mythological figures. It would take forever, and he wouldn't believe her.

But she would wager, if she or someone at Claus & Company tracked down his genealogy, they would find that he was a relation several times removed from one of the royal families, the ones that spawned all the Charmings of fairy tale myths.

Not that he would know that or even believe it.

She waved her hand dismissively, and didn't do any magic at that moment. She shook her head at the same time.

"None of this matters," she said. "I like you. You like me, and we're just not suited. You'll never believe me, not that it really matters, because ultimately, you're grounded in this world, and my feet are firmly planted in a different one."

His eyes narrowed. "Grounded in this world?"

"You have family here, and friends, and students who probably adore you, and classes to teach, things to do that you loved so much you couldn't wait to return to them. Or your university. Whereas I am in Manhattan much of the time, and the rest of the time, I'm in the North Pole—not the one the British kept trying to conquer in the 19th century, but the one you see on television specials and in kids' books, the one that's replicated in every mall in American starting just after Thanksgiving—"

"If we're lucky," he muttered. "These days it's usually Halloween."

She stopped and stared at him. He shouldn't have said that. He should continue protesting. Part of him was *listening* to her, and that surprised her. No one from the Greater World had ever listened to her before.

He dropped his gaze first. He reached for the coffee, then cupped the mug. The candy cane stir stick had melted down to half its size. When he swirled the coffee inside the mug, the cane fell all the way into the liquid.

"What if I asked you again what I asked you in the restaurant?" he said.

"You asked me what happened," she said.

"After that," he said. "I asked you to make me believe."

"You didn't know what you were asking," she said.

"Theoretically, I do now," he said.

Her heart pounded. "Why would you ask that? You think I'm crazy."

He shrugged one shoulder. He was still looking inside that coffee mug as if it held the secret to his existence.

"You know," he said, "life has never been normal for my family. It's always been—a little better than normal, at least by other people's standards. It's like the book. I wrote a public health manifesto, and I ended up all over national television. It isn't what I wanted, but it's not *normal*."

She smiled in spite of herself.

"My first girlfriend, in high school, she said that it seemed like my family led a charmed life. We were all smart, good-looking people, whom everyone liked. She said—and, looking back, I think this is pretty wise for a seventeen year-old—she said, every family had at least *one* person no one liked or who wasn't as successful or *something*. She said it was like one person took all the family's bad luck and held it, and we didn't have that person. We still don't."

Nissa tilted her head just a little. He could be...convinced? Really? She wouldn't have expected it. Although she had never tried to convince anyone in the Greater World before.

His gaze met hers. That jolt—again. She wondered if it would ever go away, and then she realized that she didn't want it to. Not ever.

Her heart twisted.

"You said that I seemed grounded here, in this place, with my university and my students. But teaching is getting repetitive. And I found myself wondering if there's anything more. That's one of the reasons I wrote the book." He sipped more of the coffee. "That kind of more, I can do without."

"Yeah," she said. "So you're not tied here."

"I love my family. But they have their own lives," he said. "And I'm *single*."

He put an emphasis on single, as if he thought she might not believe it.

"You want me to help you believe," she said.

"Yeah," he said.

"You're sure?" she asked.

"Yes," he said, and he sounded certain. But how could he be certain? He didn't know what he was asking.

She could talk him to death or she could take him home. She grabbed his right hand across the desk, and whispered, "Home, please."

And hoped that this extreme gesture would work—even though she didn't really think it would.

CHAPTER 22

*H*ER HAND WAS warm. His was too hot, from that weird coffee mug that had just appeared. And it took all of his strength not to be impressed and/or weirded out by that. He still clutched the mug in his other hand as she whispered, "Home, please."

Then snowflakes whooshed around him like a television snowstorm, perfect little cartoon flakes against a blue-black background. He felt faintly dizzy, but Nissa's hand in his steadied him. And the coffee mug. Somehow he hadn't let go of the coffee mug.

The swirling stopped, and he found himself in a too-hot living room that smelled faintly of cats. It looked like someone had vomited Christmas decorations all over the furniture—Santa blankets, red-and-green crocheted pillows, gigantic plastic candy canes on the walls along with family photos rimmed by those fake holiday frames that seemed to overrun the malls at Christmas time.

Bing Crosby and David Bowie dueted on "Little Drummer Boy," and Ryan was about to ask if this was all some kind of strange dream when a woman swore behind him.

He turned, saw a round woman with red cheeks and white hair. She held a frozen dinner in her right hand and a loaf of French bread in the other. She was looking at Nissa, who was standing beside him, not across from him like she had a moment ago.

"I wasn't going to eat the whole thing," the round woman said, as if she'd been caught doing something bad. "I just—"

"It's all right, Mother," Nissa said in a tone that implied it wasn't all right. "I didn't mean to drop in on you like this."

"I'm trying to follow the diet, honestly I am," Nissa's mother said in that defensive way that alcoholics who had been caught drinking used.

"I know, Mother," Nissa said sadly.

She squeezed Ryan's hand, then let it go. He felt the loss as if he'd lost the only real thing in the room. (Except that damn coffee mug.)

"Mother, I'd like you to meet Ryan Palmer."

Her mother smiled, and then—finally—Ryan saw the resemblance. Her mother had been stunning once, the kind of stunning Nissa was. Only her mother was shorter and had probably always been rounder, even decades ago. Her skin was lighter too, and her eyes were the same color blue his were. But that smile was spectacular. Heart-stopping. No wonder she had found love on vacation; men had probably followed her everywhere.

"The infamous Professor Palmer," her mother said. "I should have recognized you."

"Mother…" Nissa said. "When would you have seen him?"

"You think I wasn't going to watch you on television?" her mother asked. "I never miss anything you're on. Sometimes I'm late to the party, but I eventually get to see it all."

Nissa looked horrified. But her mother didn't seem to notice.

"I knew from the way you two looked at each other," her mother said, "that I'd end up meeting you eventually. I suppose this is your first time to the North Pole, Professor?"

Ryan opened his mouth and then closed it. He realized, in that second, that he could deny it all. He could shake that coffee mug at Nissa and say, *You drugged this*, and she would look at him with great disappointment. Or, he could choose to believe —and yes, it was a choice—and go with the vision. Or the truth. Or whatever this was.

"Yes," he said. "It's my first time."

"Well," her mother said, that impish smile still on her face. "I'll bet you don't believe any of this. My husband didn't on his first trip. And he froze his sexy butt off."

"*Mother*," Nissa said.

"He *did*," her mother said. "He refused to change out of his Speedo before I brought him. Didn't I tell you that?"

"No," Nissa said flatly. "You never mentioned that part."

"Oh, how your grandmother laughed," her mother said. "At least you're dressed properly, Professor."

"It's January," he said, and then remembered that people wore Speedos in Hawaii in January, which had to be what Nissa's mother was referring to. That Vacation Meet. "In New York, anyway."

"And you've decided to convince him to what?" Nissa's mother asked her. "To fall in love with you?"

His heart pounded. It couldn't be a spell could it? The way he thought about Nissa? That wasn't magic was it?

"Mother, I don't have that kind of magic, and if I did—"

"It's too late anyway," Ryan said.

They both looked at him. Nissa looked like she was about to cry. He realized in that moment that she believed he was going to demand to return to New York, to get out of this craziness, to be somewhere else.

"I think," he said, because he decided it was time to tell the truth, no matter what he believed. "I think I'm in love with you already."

CHAPTER 23

*N*ISSA HADN'T EXPECTED it. Especially now, in her mother's too-hot living room near the frozen dinner that would probably contribute to her mother's early death. The cats were hiding, it was snowing outside, and Bing Crosby's last Christmas album was on a loop. Apparently, her mother had been feeling down.

She wasn't down any more. She was trying not to laugh. Her eyes twinkled, like any good elf's eyes did when they were extremely happy.

"I just want you to know we can't do that kind of magic spell," Nissa said. "It's not possible—it's black magic, dark magic, and the Pole neutralizes—"

"Shut up, child," her mother said. "He didn't ask."

Nissa would have asked. She had a hunch he thought of asking. But he hadn't asked. He *hadn't* asked.

"You believe me?" Nissa said.

"About the magic?" he said. "Either this is the most vivid dream I've ever had, or there's more in this world than dreamt of in your philosophy, Horatio."

"*Hamlet*," her mother said, clasping her hands together. "You found a man who quotes *Hamlet*."

"Only when I'm rattled," Ryan said.

Her mother's laughter trilled through the room. Nissa smiled as well.

"Oh, for heaven's sake," her mother said. "Kiss him already."

Nissa glanced at him, then decided *not* to take her mother's advice. Because the kind of kissing she wanted to do was the kind of kissing a woman did not do in front of her mother.

Nissa sent that message to Ryan with her eyes, and he seemed to get it, because he smiled at her.

"So," he said, "is this the entire North Pole or is there more to show me?"

"There's an entire world to show you," she said. "May I borrow some coats, Mother?"

"Be my guest," her mother said. And then she touched Ryan's arm. "Welcome to our little corner of the universe, Professor Charming."

"That's not my—"

"Don't even try," Nissa said. "Mother's magical ability is to identify magic. She was calling you that for my benefit. I figured it out on my own, Mother."

"Hmm," her mother said. "There's hope for you yet."

Nissa grabbed two coats and hustled Ryan outdoors. The air was no colder than it had been in Manhattan that morning, but the snow was drier. It crunched under their feet.

This part of the village glowed yellow with artificial light. Contrary to myth and television legend, no one had Christmas lights on here year round. If they could have made the place into a tropical paradise in January, someone would have done so.

"Sorry about my mother," she said.

"Don't apologize," he said. "She's the one who convinced me."

"Convinced you of what?" Nissa asked as she stopped on the path.

"That this is real. She loves you. I can feel it. And she's lonely."

"Yeah," Nissa said. "She is."

He threaded his fingers through hers. "I'll be honest. I'm deeply and thoroughly freaked out by all of this. And, at the same time, it feels right."

"It does?" she asked.

"Like I've known it all along," he said.

She smiled. "That's just because of the myths and legends."

"I actually suspect the commercialization of Christmas. My favorite movie as a child was *Miracle on 34th Street*."

"No, it wasn't," she said.

"Yes, it was," he said. "I always wanted Santa to walk into my life. And now, apparently, he can."

She felt that tightness in her heart. Was he here for Santa then—

"And no, it's not about Santa," he said. "it's about magic. I've always believed that love is a form of magic. The kind you get in real life."

"It is," she whispered. "Just not love spells."

"I know," he said. "Speaking of, you've left me hanging."

"What?" she asked.

He paused for a half second before he spoke. "Your mother said you should kiss me."

But that was obviously not what he had meant to say. He'd declared his love for her, and she hadn't said anything in return.

She wrapped her fingers through his. Somewhere along the way, he had set down that silly coffee mug. Probably on one of her mother's over-decorated tables.

"When I was little," she said, "and I heard my parents talk

about how fast they fell in love, I didn't believe them. I told my mother I would never bring anyone here unprepared."

"Yet you brought me," he said.

She nodded. "Because I love you. And I didn't expect to."

"I thought you were trying to drive me away," he said.

"I was," she said. "I was so afraid that if you rejected me or what I am that I couldn't take it. But I can't lie to you, Ryan. From the moment I met you, I couldn't. And believe me, surviving in the Greater World requires a lot of finesse."

"You don't live here, then?" he asked.

"I prefer New York," she said.

He smiled. "We come from two different worlds."

"No kidding," she said.

"I meant, I'm a professor and you're a media consultant."

"Image Specialist," she said.

"I stand corrected. Image Specialist," he said. "Those worlds are very different."

"As different as this one and the Greater World," she said.

"Maybe even more so," he said. "But I've been thinking about it. I want to keep teaching. Just in a different way."

"Meaning?"

"I don't know," he said, and then looked around the area. "I think I have a lot to learn."

"I think you have a lot to teach," she said. "The people here need to understand how media image has an impact on lives."

"I'm not a media consultant," he said, his fingers loose in hers. She liked the feel of them against hers.

"But you have a lot to say," she said, "and it's sensible."

He sighed. "It doesn't look like I belong here."

"We need you," she said. "My mother needs you, and everyone like her. They need to change some things about their lives—"

"No one likes a nag," he said, and she winced. Then he

frowned. "Is that what your mother meant when you came? That you've been—"

"Oh, don't say it," she said. "She's got so many health problems."

He turned so that he could face her, keeping his hand entwined with hers. "That's what you meant about teach?"

She nodded. "I'm losing this fight. I'm losing *her*."

"But the magic—"

"Doesn't stop death," she said.

He looked both startled and sad.

"We can work together," she said. "I can help with imagery back home, and you can help with education here."

"Back home," he said. "Isn't this home?"

She made herself smile. "New York is home for me."

"I know you live there, but—

"It's *home*," she said. "I don't think I can live here anymore."

He pulled her closer. "So if we—are—together, then we live—?"

"In the United States," she said. And wondered if that disappointed him.

He smiled. His wonderful eyes started to twinkle. "We'd have both worlds?"

"Yes," she said, "and I can explain them to you."

"Good," he said. "Because I want to hear all about this. After you fulfill your promise to me."

It was her turn to smile. And then she leaned in for the kiss. It was the kind of kiss no one gave in front of their mother. It was deep and passionate and warmed her right up.

"I have an apartment in Manhattan," she said.

"Not here?" he asked against her lips.

"A room in my mother's house," she said.

"Can we get back to New York?" he asked.

"Your wish…" she started, but he put a finger on her lips.

"Don't say it," he said. "That's too close to *I Dream of Jeanne* to me, and that show creeped me out."

"You have magic too," she said.

"But I don't know how to use it," he said.

"Oh," she said as she spelled them back to her Manhattan apartment, "yes, you do."

EPILOGUE

*H*E COULD CHARM her mother. Ryan could charm anyone, but the fact that he could charm Nissa's mother surprised Nissa more than she could admit. He was the one who figured out that her mother wouldn't go to Greater World doctors because Nissa had wanted to take her to New York.

He simply said they should go to Hawaii, and have her mother see doctors there.

Of course, he didn't tell her mother that. He told her mother that she would be attending a wedding.

Which she did.

After her doctor's appointments.

And Nissa's entire Hawaiian family showed up, along with Ryan's family—charming people all. The wedding didn't even feel cobbled together, although it took place in February, and his family seemed to think it had all happened fast.

Maybe. But she was getting used to fast. She had fallen for him fast. He said he had fallen for her fast. And they had progressed from disbelief to belief to *oh, my God, this is fantastic* in the space of an afternoon.

Waiting a month for a wedding seemed like an eternity.

They had already decided to work together. They knew they could help each other, with family, with their jobs, with their strange magicks. But she figured it would all work out.

Because he had gotten her mother to see doctors who could actually help her.

And Nissa believed that to be a miracle.

Almost on par with the miracle of meeting him.

He called it all magic.

And, she had to admit, he was absolutely right.

KRISTINE GRAYSON

Dressed in Holiday Style

THE SANTA SERIES

Read more in the next book in the Santa Series, *Dressed in Holiday Style,* available from your favorite bookseller. Following is a sample chapter from that book.

Once Upon a Time...
Not too long ago...but long enough to be somewhen else...

RAINE WILKINS STOOD in the ankle-deep snow, staring over the hedge. The mansion's golden interior light spilled across the massive yard. All of the trees and shrubs beside the building were covered in silver fairy lights, with a touch of red and green, tastefully placed to hint at the season. A gigantic Christmas tree stood in the floor-to-ceiling bay window of the ballroom, but the other windows—also large—revealed couples waltzing as if they were extras in a Fred Astaire movie.

The women wore long dresses that flowed with their every movement, their hair short and styled or long and piled on top of their heads, held in place with tiaras and bows and jewelry that glittered. The men wore tuxes with tails that added to the sense of motion.

She could almost hear the music.

Someday, she would dance like that. Someday, she would be invited to these glitzy, glamorous parties. Someday, she would be one of the glittering women, swirling around the dance floor as if bred for it.

She wasn't bred for it, of course. She stood in the snow, her ancient boots starting to leak, her ratty (but warm) parka wrapped around her, her gloved hands tucked inside the sleeves, creating a makeshift muff. She had forgotten a hat, and she didn't want to put the hood up because it would block her vision. The parka was heavy-duty, the kind built for a good Midwestern winter, the kind they'd had when she was a kid, the kind the weather forecasters said they would have this year.

She shouldn't be here. She had told herself she would drive to the mansion in Lincoln Park just to see how long it took to get there from her ratty apartment on the Near West Side, knowing that tomorrow she would have to account for traffic as well.

But she had known, deep down, that she wanted to see the gala event of the season and imagine herself taking part, instead of standing on the sidelines, asking questions about the event—for, of all things, the Life and Style page (which her editor snidely called "the society page").

She hated Life and Style work. But, she reminded herself, unlike her colleagues from Northwestern, she had gotten a paying job as a reporter at the *Chicago Courier*, one of the few remaining big dailies in the nation, and she'd been promised that she could keep the job if she outperformed every other new hire from that summer.

Outperforming meant taking the humiliating work along with the good stories. Not that any good stories had come her way yet. She was too young and too new.

She was covering stupid stuff—high-end engagement parties, routine political speeches, and (her least favorite) the county fair. Often, she was doing background for one of the "real" reporters, or helping them post their articles on the paper's brand-new website.

She hadn't expected this. She had awards and credentials. She had written for major newspapers (with the prodding help of her professors), and she had interned at one of the most prestigious papers in the country—for no money, of course. She'd actually had to pay the university tuition for the privilege of interning, because the position provided "experience" and "enhanced her résumé" while infusing her with more cynicism than a woman of twenty-four should probably have.

She sighed. She wished, just once, she had some money and respect. She knew that the very rich people waltzing inside that mansion weren't the stuff of fairy tales, but she liked to imagine they were. The Rich—different from everyone else, if she were to believe F. Scott Fitzgerald. She liked to believe they not only had better clothes and more financial opportunities, but also perfect lives.

She'd never had a perfect life. She'd been so poor that she hadn't known where her next meal would come from. Not a lot of Northwestern freshman had homeless parents and full scholarships. She'd kept that secret, even from her best friends at school.

College had been a luxury for her, and her experiences growing up had enabled her to survive that disastrous internship without going either hungry or bankrupt.

She'd even freelanced. That had made her so much more money than her stupid job was earning her right now. Maybe she should give up the steady paycheck and strike out on her own....

"Aren't you cold?"

The male voice from behind her made her jump. Her heart rate increased a thousandfold, but she tried to pretend she wasn't alarmed as she turned to see who spoke.

A tall, blond man stood behind her. He was about her age, with flawless skin—the type she would have killed for—just starting to pink up from the chill, a square jaw, and blue eyes so electric they seemed lit from within.

Men this handsome didn't just lurk behind shrubbery. Particularly men this handsome who were also wearing a tux as if they'd been born to it.

The white scarf wrapped around his neck appeared to be his only concession to the weather. He had his hands in the pockets of his tux trousers, but he didn't look cold.

She wondered if he was drunk.

"I feel like I should be offering you my parka," she said. "Isn't that the chivalrous thing to do?"

He shrugged one broad shoulder. "The chill feels good. It's stuffy inside."

"It'll feel good for a few minutes," she said. "And then you're going to regret you ever stepped out here."

"And regret that I joined you to spy on the Lifestyles of the Rich and Famous?" He didn't sound sarcastic, but in her mind, she could hear Robin Leach's smarmy voice blaring the words. She hadn't thought of that show since she was a kid. Even then, it had been a guilty pleasure.

Her cheeks heated. She'd been caught.

She decided not to lie. "It looks pretty in there."

"Oh," he said. "It is pretty, in a soulless, let's-make-this-the-most-stunning-room-in-the-world sort of way."

As if she knew what that was. She'd like to experience it, just once.

"You don't like it," she said, both as a question and a statement.

He shrugged again, his blue eyes looking past her. He was taller than she was. He could probably see inside so much better than she could.

"I've always liked that saying, 'Home is where the heart is,'" he said.

Something about the way he spoke the cliché caught her ear. She'd been concentrating so hard on not looking startled by him that she hadn't noticed, until now, that he had one of those indefinable European accents. An English-is-my-second-language-and-I-speak-it-better-than-you accent.

"You'd better go back inside before you freeze," she said.

He smiled faintly and looked at the windows. Their light reflected in his magnificent eyes.

"I'm not sure I'm going back in," he said.

She frowned. "Why not?"

He shrugged again. "I have a hunch," he said softly, "I'm about to run away."

I value honest feedback, and would love to hear your opinion in a review, if you're so inclined, on your favorite book retailer's site.

Be the first to know!

Just sign up for the Kristine Kathryn Rusch newsletter, and keep up with the latest news, releases and so much more—even the occasional giveaway.

So, what are you waiting for? To sign up go to kristinekathrynrusch.com.

But wait! There's more. Sign up for the WMG Publishing newsletter, too, and get the latest news and releases from all of the WMG authors and lines, including Kristine Grayson, Kris Nelscott, Dean Wesley Smith, *Fiction River: An Original Anthology Magazine, Smith's Monthly,* and so much more.

To sign up go to wmgpublishing.com.

ABOUT THE AUTHOR

Called "The Reigning Queen of Paranormal Romance" by *Best Reviews,* bestselling author Kristine Grayson has made a name for herself publishing light, slightly off-skew romance novels about Greek Gods, fairy tale characters, and the modern world.

She writes historical mysteries as Kris Nelscott, and she also writes in a variety of genre, from literary to science fiction to romance, under her real name—Kristine Kathryn Rusch. She has won dozens of awards for her writing

As Kristine Grayson, she also edits the romance volumes of *Fiction River: An Original Anthology Magazine.*

For more information about her work, go to the Kristine Grayson www.kristinegrayson.com and sign up for her newsletter.